MORE
SECRET LIVES OF
CHANDLERS FORD

Stories written by:
Maggie Farran,
Catherine Griffin,
Sally Howard,
Karen Stephen.

ISBN: 153960702X
ISBN-13: 978-1539607021

Cover design: Sally Howard
Photography: Emily Howard, John Farran

The stories in this collection reference
real locations in Chandler's Ford.
However, all characters and events are
entirely fictional.

The Authors

From left to right: Sally Howard, Catherine Griffin, Maggie Farran, and Karen Stephen

About the Authors

The writers met at a local creative writing class several years ago. Keen to develop their hobby, they formed a writing group to discuss story ideas and read their work to each other. After several meetings consisting of coffee, cake, and gossip, the idea for a collection of fictional short stories set in and around Chandler's Ford was born.

Sally is originally from the Midlands. She is a working mother of daughters and two naughty kittens. Sally enjoys writing for children and young adults. She unwinds by cooking and reading (sometimes at the same time, with mixed results).

Catherine hails from Bristol. After working as a software engineer, she is now a full-time writer of fantasy novels. She enjoys writing contemporary stories with a twist. She is a keen gardener.

Maggie is a former Chandler's Ford teacher. Her stories are gentle, family-centred, and often romantic. Maggie adores spending time with her children and grandchildren. She enjoys voluntary work and sings in a local choir.

Karen moved to Chandler's Ford for a work project. Eighteen years later, she's still here. She works full-time. She enjoys writing across several genres including historical and contemporary stories. Karen loves theatre, books, and socialising.

It has been an incredible, thrilling experience to write, publish, and market the book. We hope you have as much fun reading it as we did it bringing it to you.

Contents

Forgive Me, They Were Delicious

Sally Howard

The sun sets in a blaze of glory, at the end of a hot summer's day. It's going to be another fabulous day tomorrow, I think as I stomp through the trampled grass, my dress snagging on tent pegs, my feet sweating and smelly in wellies.

It's all Adam's fault.

'Booked for Boomtown again.' He flapped the tickets in my face, all eager-beaver that he was among the first to book. 'Excellent pitch. Near our usual spot.'

I stop for a minute, tucking my wash bag under my arm, watching the last rays of the sun dip behind smoky pink-tipped clouds. I remember our first festival. We'd not being going out for long. I'd mentioned how I'd always wanted to go to a festival. Adam had surprised me by buying tickets. It'd been so exciting, getting kitted out, visiting Go Outdoors down in Southampton and snuggling into their pop-up tents.

But compact and bijou, instant pitch tents have lost their appeal. Is it too much to ask to go on a proper holiday? Stay in a room? Not have negotiate my way through a field of tents to a water tap?

The last straw is Adam leaving my bag behind, with my summer shoes in it. He'd spent enough time faffing around with the icebox, making sure he'd packed his precious plums. Great, so now all I have to wear on my feet are these stomping swamp-green rubber monstrosities. Sweaty and damp inside, my feet itch terribly. When I reach the taps, I'm going to wash my feet under cool water before having to put on those dratted wellies again.

It's dark by the time I'm finished. As I start to trace my way back, I wonder whether Adam will have returned to the tent. We'd both stormed off after rowing about the bag. At this moment, I really don't care where he's gone or when he gets back.

I nearly collide with someone coming out of the bar.

'Hey, girl with the wellies.' The guy smiles, brown eyes warm in the glow of the lamplight.

'I've seen you walk this way before.' His eyes flicker down my body, stopping at my cumbersome foot attire. 'In your wellies.'

I feel my cheeks glow red.

When I don't reply, he chuckles. 'You look like you could use a drink, and I've just been stood up, so how about it?'

I consider the path back to a dark, cramped tent. One drink won't matter, will it?

Laughing, drunk, we stumble back to my tent. It's dark. No sign of Adam.

'Nice tent,' says warm brown eyes, who is called Jake. He pulls open the zip and peers inside. 'Roomy.'

I giggle. I haven't laughed so much in ages. He's been doing wicked impressions of the bands that were playing today, over a glass of beer or three.

'Got any food?' he says.

'Um, not much. Hang on, we have plums!' We fall about laughing, though I don't quite know why this is so funny.

We stagger round to the back of the tent and I open the icebox. My mouth waters in anticipation of the sweet juiciness of the plums. There are only two left, saved for the last morning. I pull one out, plump and round, and place it in the palm of his hand. He lifts the plum to his lips and bites into it. Purple juice oozes down his chin. He wipes it with his finger, then licks the juice off with his tongue.

He watches me with intense brown eyes. I bite into mine. It's cool and sweet. I lick my lips to catch the juice before it runs down my chin. He leans in. I smell the same sweetness on his breath, the same sweetness in his mouth, as his lips close on mine. My head spins and a warmth, like chocolate, steals into my stomach.

Some moments later, I draw back gently and shake my head.

'I'm sorry, I can't.'

I run my finger over the back of his hand. 'I'm really very drunk and you're very nice. But I've made a mistake.'

He nods, shrugs, stands up.

'I can tell you're a nice girl.' As he walks away, he winks. 'You change your mind any time, we can still make music.'

I unzip the tent and crawl in, leaving the dratted wellies at the entrance. Slipping into my sleeping bag, I perform my well-practised undressing manoeuvre in the dark. Slipping on my warm socks against the cool night air, I think about Jake. What a gentleman. Jake. I roll the name around on my tongue.

But Adam and I have been going out for three years now. That's some investment in our relationship. We've had good times together. Are we just stuck in a rut?

Jake made me laugh. I giggle again at one of his jokes. Should I have...? Oh, it's all so complicated!

With that thought, I fall asleep.

'Hey, sleepy head.'

Sunlight filters through the tent walls in a greenish glow. I groan and roll over. It feels like a band is tuning up inside my head.

Adam unzips the tent from the outside and leans in.

'Hey,' he says. 'I come bringing gifts. A latte and blueberry muffin.'

The smile fades from his eyes and his brow creases.

'Look, I'm sorry I forgot the bag. I'm sorry I went out drinking last night and left you alone in the tent. Peace offering?' He holds up the cup, steam curling from the plastic lid. 'Queued for half an hour for this.'

I smile, tentatively. 'Double latte?'

'Yep, double latte.'

'Skinny muffin?'

'The very one.'

'I'm sorry too.'

He props the paper-plated muffin and coffee cup on the sleeping bag beside me and crawls into the tent.

'And also,' he says. 'I know you're fed up with coming here. I've been thinking. Let's book a proper holiday next year.'

'Oh, Adam.' I throw my arms around him. 'I love you.'

'I love you too.'

Released from my embrace, he hands me my coffee. I take a sip and wait for the caffeine to kick in. Never mind the wellies, today is gonna be a lovely day, just me and Adam.

Adam pushes himself towards the door.

'I'll just get our last two plums from the icebox, then you can tell me what you did last night.'

Chandler's Ford Station

Maggie Farran

19th October 2003

'Charlie Dimmock is going to be there. You know, that lady gardener off the TV. She wears all those skimpy T-shirts and never wears a bra. All the men love watching her do her digging,' said Chloe, trying to grab the hand of her four-year-old son, Joe.

Miranda laughed. 'I wouldn't miss the official reopening of Chandler's Ford station. I can't believe it's actually happened at last. It's great to have our own station again after all these years. It's so much easier going into Southampton now I don't have to go on the bus. Cheaper too.'

Her son, Ben, trotted along beside her. Both little boys clutched model steam trains.

They ambled along Park Road towards the newly-built station enjoying the autumn day. Joe, with his curly red hair, ran on ahead, with Ben trying to keep up with him.

'We're going to see a train, we're going to see a train,' the boys chanted together.

'Stop at the curb, Joe,' Chloe shouted. 'He's such a dare devil. I never know what he's going to do next. There's going to be a real steam train there for the opening. The boys will love it. They're old enough now. It's great that they're such good friends although they are so different.'

'Ben would have *Thomas the Tank Engine* as his bedtime story every night if he got his way,' laughed Miranda. 'It doesn't seem like four years since we met up in Winchester Maternity Unit. I would have gone mad without you, Chloe.'

'Don't be daft, Miranda. You're a great Mum. You're too hard on yourself.'

Miranda felt pleased that Chloe saw her as a success. The last four years had been quite a struggle, managing her son, Ben, on her own. She really didn't know how she would have coped without Chloe's friendship. She was so upbeat and encouraging.

Chloe had a kind, supportive husband, Tom, to help her bring up Joe. Miranda couldn't help feeling a little envious. Ben's father had disappeared as soon as he heard the news of her pregnancy. When Ben was first born she'd sent him photos of his chubby little son, but she never heard anything from him in response.

They arrived at the station and climbed up the stairs and onto the bridge. They looked down at the track that stretched between Eastleigh and Romsey. Ben and Joe trotted down the stairs on the other side to the gleaming new platform. There was quite a crowd waiting for the steam train to arrive from Eastleigh. Miranda took hold of Ben's hand. Chloe and little Joe stood beside them as they watched the gleaming dark green steam train glide majestically into the station.

'Look, boys, it says UNION OF SOUTH AFRICA on it. Look at all that steam,'said Miranda

Ben and Joe beamed at each other in delight.

'They can't believe they're seeing a real steam train at last,' shouted Chloe, trying to be heard over the sound of the train.

After the crowd had given it many admiring glances the train set out from the station towards Romsey in a cloud of steam. Miranda was lost in her memories of *The Railway Children*. The part where Roberta sees her father through the clearing steam had always moved her to tears. She was jolted into the present day by Chloe.

'Where's Joe, Miranda?'

Miranda looked around her. He had been standing beside them a minute ago, looking at the train. He couldn't be far away.

Miranda held Ben's hand tightly and asked, 'Sweetheart, have you any idea where Joe has gone?'

Ben looked down at the ground and shrugged.

She and Chloe looked around them calmly at first and then grew more and more terrified. There was absolutely no sign of him on the platform or in the station. They went outside to where a crowd was gathered round watching Charlie Dimmock digging enthusiastically, her breasts joining in the action, ready to plant the special tree in memory of the occasion.

Miranda and Chloe raced around the crowd asking 'Has anyone seen a little boy? He's four and he's holding a model of Thomas the Tank Engine.'

There was absolutely no sign of him. He seemed to have vanished. They rushed up the stairs to the bridge and down the other side.

'What am I going to tell his Dad? Do you think I should ring him now? Do you think I should ring the police?' gabbled Chloe.

'Give it a minute. I'm sure he'll turn up in a second or two. Look, down there I can see some red hair in the crowd.'

They ran across the bridge and back to the platform. The red-haired child turned round. It wasn't Joe, but another boy of about the same age.

'He must be somewhere. He can't just have disappeared.' Miranda put her arm round Chloe and squeezed her shoulder.

Chloe looked grey with desperation. 'I feel icy cold and my brain doesn't seem to be working properly. I've lost Joe. What am I going to do?'

Miranda helped Chloe into the station as if she were an old lady. Chloe's legs didn't seem to belong to her.

'I'll talk to one of the staff, Chloe. I'll tell them what's happened. Maybe we should ring Tom and the police. It's been over five minutes now.'

Chloe sat on the hard plastic seat and shivered. 'Do you think someone has stolen him? You hear such awful things happening to young children.'

Quite a crowd of people were now joining in the search, calling Joe's name. Ben clung to Miranda's hand terrified by all the fuss and the loss of his best friend.

'Where's Joe gone, Mummy? Why is everyone shouting his name?'

'We don't know where Joe is, sweetie. Everyone is trying to help us find him.'

Ben rubbed a tear away with the back of his hand.

Suddenly a young policewoman tapped Chloe on the shoulder.

'We hear you've lost your little boy. Well, we've just heard from Romsey Station that a little boy got on the train by himself at

Chandler's Ford. Apparently he sat with a family group and no one realised he was on his own until the train arrived in Romsey. Don't worry, he's safe and well. He's in a police car now on his way back here.'

Chloe hugged Miranda and burst into tears.

'Oh, thank goodness. I never thought in my wildest dreams that he would get on a train by himself. I suppose with all that steam we didn't notice him climbing on the train. I'm the worst mother ever.'

'Of course you're not, Chloe. I was there too and I didn't notice either. I always think you're a wonderful Mum. You're always doing lovely activities with Joe. Don't beat yourself up. It could have happened to anyone.'

After a long quarter of an hour a police car pulled up outside the station and a beaming Joe got out.

'Mummy, I've been on a steam train and now I've been in a police car. This is the best day of my life.'

Chloe hugged her son tightly.

She whispered to Miranda, 'It's has been the worst day of my life. I don't know what I would have done without you. I just fell to pieces. You were so calm all the time. Thanks so much. You're such a wonderful friend to me.'

That evening Miranda read *Thomas the Tank Engine* for the third time to Ben. He gave her such a lovely smile as she kissed him goodnight.

'Mum, can we go on that train one day?' he whispered.

'Yes sweetheart, maybe not that actual train, but we could go on the train to visit Grandma. We would have to go on two trains to get to London, but I'm sure we could manage it together. You are such a big, sensible boy now.'

With Ben safely asleep upstairs. Miranda poured herself a large glass of sparkling white wine and curled up on the sofa to read her own book, which didn't mention trains. She and Ben were going to be just fine.

The Quiet Neighbour
Catherine Griffin

Sandra had just sat down to enjoy MasterChef when the doorbell buzzed. She glared at her husband's currently empty corner of the sofa, then at the dog.

'Whoever can *that* be at *this* time of night?'

Goldie thumped her tail on the carpet. When the doorbell buzzed again, followed by a sharp knock, Sandra dragged herself from the sofa cushions. With Goldie panting on her heels, she went to the front door.

She hesitated, her fingers resting on the cold metal of the latch. Imagination populated the darkness outside with desperate masked men. Such things did happen, after all. You heard such horror stories on the news. Not in Chandler's Ford though, and Miles was only upstairs. Even engrossed in his toy soldiers, he'd probably notice if she screamed in terror. Not that he'd be much use in a crisis. It was hardly likely to be burglars anyway – probably one of the neighbours wanted to borrow something.

She opened the door a couple of inches. On the doorstep stood a dark figure holding a package. He coughed.

'Excuse me. I have a delivery for next door, but he doesn't seem to be in. Would you mind...?'

The orange glow of the street lamp caught the young man's clean-shaven face. Automatically, she took the parcel he offered. Next door's address was scrawled across the brown paper wrapping in black marker pen.

'For Mr Brown?'

'It's urgent. Can you see he gets it as soon as possible?'

She had closed the door and turned away before it occurred to her that packages weren't usually delivered that late in the evening. At least, when Miles ordered something or other from the internet, which seemed to be nearly every day, his purchases always appeared in daylight. She peered at the package, looking for a courier's label. There was none. No stamps, no nothing. Just the hand-written address.

'Who was that at the door?' Miles said from the top of the stairs.

He started down, wiping his hands on a red-stained cloth.

'Just a delivery. For Mr Brown.'

She frowned at the parcel. It was heavier than the size suggested, and solid. Maybe books? Miles took it from her, hefting it curiously.

'Mr Brown's gone away,' he said.

'Away? How long for?'

He shrugged. 'I saw him loading luggage into his car yesterday. He said he was going away, might be gone for some time.'

'And you were going to mention this when?'

'Thought I had. Didn't I?' He took off his glasses and wiped his brow with the cloth, leaving a streak of red paint on his cheek.

'No, you didn't.'

14

Goldie snuffled at the package. She'd had a bit of a parcel obsession since the kids got her doggie chocolates one Christmas. Sandra pushed her away.

'Well, what do we with this, if he's away?'

'There's no return address.' Miles turned the package over and shook it experimentally. 'Nothing we can do, really. I dare say he'll turn up eventually.'

He dropped the parcel on the hall table by the phone. And there it stayed, as days passed into weeks.

It wasn't unusual for Mr Brown to be away from home. He travelled several times a year, often for weeks at a time. Sandra assumed it was business. What kind of business, she didn't know, but clearly he had money. Houses in this street weren't cheap, and in the few years he'd lived next door a succession of expensive new black cars had occupied his driveway.

He didn't seem to have family and rarely had visitors. She suspected he was foreign only because he spoke like BBC news presenters used to, with deliberate precision and no accent at all. He was always polite on the rare occasions when they met but kept himself to himself. In many ways, the perfect neighbour.

But now, each time she passed the parcel in the hall, sitting beside the phone under Michael's graduation photo, it brought a tickle of doubt.

Then one day, it wasn't there.

She wandered into the kitchen to see Miles staring at the parcel in his hands, with Goldie sitting at attention in front of him.

'Have you developed X-ray vision or are you having a stroke?'

'It was getting dusty in the hall. Thought I'd put it out of the way. Then I started thinking...'

'Never a good idea.'

'Maybe we should open it.'

Strange how you could live with someone for thirty years and still be surprised by how their brain worked.

'We can't do that,' she said.

'What if he never comes back?'

'So? It still isn't *our* parcel.'

He had that mulish look he got when he knew he was wrong but didn't want to admit it. She reached for the package. He pulled it away from her.

Goldie, presumably concluding in her little dog brain that this was a general game of grab-the-parcel, jumped up and sunk her teeth into the brown paper.

'Let go of that! Down! Bad dog!' Sandra seized her collar.

Miles jerked the parcel out of the dog's reach, but the damage was already done. The wrapping was ripped from a bottom corner. Blue paper poked out of the hole.

'This,' Miles said, 'is not books.'

It definitely wasn't books. What it was, was a stack of twenty pound notes.

Sandra made coffee. They sat at the kitchen table with the ripped parcel between them.

'Well. Now what do we do?' Sandra said.

'We have to go to the police.'

'Do we? I mean, we don't know...?'

'No, we don't know. But *normal* people don't have bundles of money delivered to their house.'

He picked up the parcel and ripped away what was left of the wrapping.

'What are you doing? Leave it alone.' Sandra froze in horror as bundles of money flooded the table.

'It was already open. We may as well see what we're dealing with,' he said matter-of-factly, as if it were a plumbing problem.

He stacked the bundles, building a fort around himself as he counted.

'Wow. That's a lot of money. A nice holiday. A new car...'

'A big pile of lead soldiers?'

He shrugged. 'Or shoes. Each to their own.'

'It isn't our money! And it's probably stolen. Or something. You're right, we have to go to the police.'

'Hold on. Let's think this through.' He folded his arms, though his eyes never left the money. 'If Mr Brown is a criminal —'

She snorted. 'If?'

'Well, let's say he is, and we go to the police. He'll know it was us.'

'You think he could be dangerous?' Even if Mr Brown was a criminal, she couldn't imagine him doing anything violent. He was always so clean.

'Maybe not himself, but I bet he knows people. Do you remember the cherry tree?'

Just after Mr Brown had moved in, they'd mentioned to him that the cherry tree in his back garden had grown rather large. It shadowed their patio. Maybe he would consider pruning it? It hadn't been a complaint even, more a polite inquiry.

Two days later, the old cherry tree was reduced to a stump and pile of wood chip.

At the time they thought it was a little odd, but were pleased to have a sunnier garden. Now it seemed rather more sinister.

Sandra shuddered. 'It was just a tree. Besides, the police would protect us.'

'Really? He knows everything about us. We don't know anything about him.'

'You read too many crime thrillers.'

He reached across the table and took her hand. 'Look, nothing's happened, nothing will happen. I'm sure. But maybe we should just put the money away, and forget the whole business? It's not our problem. If he ever shows up, he can have it.'

His hand folded around hers, warm and comforting in its strength. And slightly sticky.

'What's this blue on your hands?'

'Oh.' He released her to inspect his palms. 'I was painting French Infantry earlier.'

He smiled at the stains fondly. It had been a long time since he looked at her that way.

Miles put the money in a biscuit tin, which he hid behind the dog food, and life went on as normal.

Two weeks passed with no reason to think about the disturbing contents of the biscuit tin, though Sandra often did in the quiet reaches of the night, while Miles lay snoring.

'Have you noticed the white van parked across the road?' Miles said, one day during lunch at the kitchen table.

'Should I have?'

'It's been there a couple of days. Different places.'

'So? Someone's always having building work done. We could do with a new kitchen ourselves.' If we had the money, she added silently.

'The bins were moved yesterday.'

She stared at him. 'You don't mean... You think someone's watching? Us?'

'Or him.' He took another big bite of sandwich.

'That's it. Enough. We have to go to the police.'

'It might be the police. Or Interpol. Or the FBI.'

'Don't be daft. The FBI are American. You mean MI5. Or is it MI6?'

'MI5, I think.'

She clutched her coffee mug as if it was an island of sanity. 'They might think we're involved, if we don't tell the police.'

'Or they might never know we have the money, if we sit tight.'

'Miles...' She wanted to say she was scared, but the words caught in her throat. How could he sit there and wolf down bread and processed cheese, as if nothing was wrong?

He cleared the lunch things, then puttered off to paint another unit of French cavalry. She peeked through the curtains in the front room at the white van, then retreated to the kitchen, only to be magnetically drawn back to the view of the street.

No one sat in the van. No one got in or got out. Twenty times she told herself off for being paranoid, and twenty times started on long-put-off chores which she didn't finish. Five o'clock found her frantically scrubbing the inside of the oven door, without noticeable effect. When she gave up and crept back to the front room, the van had gone. Limp with relief, she stared for a long time as the street darkened and the lamps came on.

When a figure loomed over her and slipped an arm around her

waist, she nearly jumped out of her skin.

'Miles! Don't do that.'

He landed a sloppy kiss on her neck before releasing her. 'They've gone. I saw from upstairs.'

'You see? It was just builders or something. You've had me panicking all day over nothing.'

'Shall I open a bottle of wine?'

'I knew I married you for a reason.'

From the back of the house, Goldie barked. They looked at each other. Sandra clutched Miles' arm.

'Someone's at the back door.'

Goldie barked again.

'Is it locked?' she said.

'No.'

'What do we do?' They were whispering, though she wasn't sure why.

'Stay here.' Miles drew himself up and headed down the hall.

Deciding she preferred to be terrified with him than terrified alone, she followed. Goldie still barked, her low gruff warning bark. Someone rapped on the double-glazed back door.

Miles stopped at the open kitchen door to peer in. Sandra crowded on his heels.

'Can you see anyone?'

'He's outside.'

She relaxed slightly. It seemed unlikely someone intending to murder them would knock on the back door and wait to be let in.

They crept into the gloomy kitchen. Goldie padded over, tail wagging, pleased with herself. Through the glass panel of the back door, a familiar profile swung into view, lit by the security light.

Sandra gripped Miles' arm. 'Mr Brown!'

He'd already spotted them, and waved.

Miles straightened up from the stealthy crouch he'd adopted. 'Well. We'd better say hello.'

When he opened the door, Mr Brown smiled his usual polite half-smile. He looked the same as ever: same neat trimmed beard, same suit, perhaps a little rumpled.

'Good evening. I hope I'm not disturbing you. May I come in?'

He slipped into the house, not exactly furtively, but with an air of relief.

'I believe you have something for me?'

Miles and Sandra exchanged glances. He raised his eyebrows. She frowned, then went to the dog food cupboard to get the tin.

With Goldie panting in her ear, she retrieved it from its hiding place. It was heavier than she remembered. All that money... And Mr Brown's mild, curious expression.

'Umm. There was a bit of an accident. We didn't mean to look.' She thrust the tin into his hands. 'It's all there.'

If he was concerned or surprised, he didn't show it. He set the tin on the kitchen table and levered off the lid. The neat bundles of money glistened under the fluorescent light.

'It's I who should apologise. You've been put in a very difficult position. Your discretion is much appreciated.' He began transferring bundles of notes to his pockets.

'Hold on just a moment,' Miles said in the firm voice he usually brought out only to send his steak back. 'If there's something criminal going on...'

'Oh my.' Another bundle of money disappeared inside his jacket. 'I see why you might be concerned, but it's nothing like that. Some of my business associates are a little... unconventional. That's all. We had a bit of a communication problem.'

He patted the bulges in his jacket. About half the money remained in the biscuit tin.

'And now, I'm afraid I must go.'

'But... what about the rest of the money?'

He paused, framed by the open back door. 'Consider it a parting gift. I don't think we'll meet again. Farewell.'

With that, he closed the door behind him and vanished into the dusk.

Miles and Sandra sat at the kitchen table.

'Wow.' She shook her head. 'To think how worried we were. Look at this... we can get the kitchen done.'

'I can't believe you're that gullible. Obviously he's up to something fishy. The money's meant to keep us quiet.'

'So? It's a bit late to go to the police now. And the money would come in handy.'

He shook his head. 'What are we going to do with it? You can't just walk into a bank with a biscuit tin full of twenties. People will ask questions. If it was stolen, the notes can be traced.'

'If we spent it in small amounts...'

'No. Just no. It's dirty money. I don't want any part of it.'

She sighed. 'Fine. You're right. I know you're right... It's just...'

'I know you want a new kitchen, but this isn't the way.'

'You're the one who's always spending. How many soldiers does one man need?'

He jammed the lid back onto the tin, and opened the bottle of wine.

Early next morning, Miles started a bonfire in the back garden.

Sandra joined him, shivering in her anorak and wellington boots.

'Are you sure about this? It seems... wrong.'

'No.' He poked the smouldering twigs. 'Do you have a better idea?'

He opened the tin, and one by one fed the bundles of money to the fire. Orange flames edged with red danced higher as the paper blackened and curled. She watched them burn, heart aching.

'New car.' He threw another bundle into the heart of the blaze. 'Holiday.'

'Stop that.'

He hesitated before the last bundle went into the fire. 'Right. It's done. All gone.'

She took his hands and kissed him on the cheek.

'What was that for?'

'I love you, and I'm proud of you.'

He pulled her close and kissed her, and for a moment they were one, wreathed in wood smoke and papery ashes.

'Does that mean I can order some Prussian infantry?'

'Don't push your luck.' She punched him in the arm. 'We're poor, remember?'

They walked back to the house. Only when he'd disappeared upstairs did she retrieve the package she'd tucked in the darkest corner of the cupboard, behind the dog food.

Goldie whuffed, wagging her tail as she watched.

'Ssh,' Sandra said. 'This is our little secret, all right? Good girl.'

Hearing Things

Karen Stephen

Wriggling her feet from her shoes, Carole sipped her tea. The lunch dishes were washed. After *Listen With Mother*, Penny had gone for her nap. Carole had thirty minutes of peace before her daughter woke up. It only seemed like yesterday since Penny was a baby. But she was "a big girl now," as Penny herself said.

Maurice had laid out her tablets as usual. Two huge yellow pellets, three times a day, after meals. He was very solicitous about it.

'Darling, Doctor Williams insisted. After your last, ahem…' He cleared his throat in that annoying way of his. '…little episode.'

Swallowing the pills, Carole vowed to stop them. They had served their purpose. The blackness she had felt after Penny's birth had long receded. The tablets dulled her senses, made everything foggy.

Thud.

There was that dratted noise again. Carole's heart raced. She placed the floral teacup on its saucer, looked at the kitchen ceiling.

Two louder thumps. She jumped. The crockery splintered as it hit the tiled floor. What would Maurice say? He had chosen the tea set. Carole had always thought it garish.

She crept to the foot of the stairs. The pendulum of the grandfather clock swung its ponderous rhythm. The ornate black hands ticked to two o'clock. The clock bonged. Carole flinched. Maurice's family heirloom. She hated the old monstrosity.

One hand on the banister, she edged up the staircase. The five white doors on the landing were closed. She tiptoed into Penny's room.

Penny lay under the coverlet, teddy clutched under one arm, cheeks rosy with sleep. Carole gently brushed fine blonde hair from her daughter's forehead. Kissed her nose.

A movement caught her eye. In the corner of the room, Penny's favourite new toy, a white crib, swayed on its rockers. Carole frowned. She had watched Penny tuck in her dolls twenty minutes ago.

Surely the cradle would have stopped rocking by now? The swaying movement made her feel drowsy.

As she took a step forward, Carole winced. Shards of pain shot through her feet. Penny's glass marbles lay scattered over the floor. She teetered, grabbing for the chest of drawers. Why were the marbles loose?

Groggy, Carole peeked into the other rooms. All the windows were closed. No visible sign of anything that could be making the noise. In their bedroom, she paused. She smoothed the floral eiderdown. Straightened the cerise curtains. It was the first room they had decorated in their new house on Park Road in the early days of their marriage. "Girly" Maurice had called it. He had been indulgent then.

A flock of magpies bickered on the lawn. She winced as three of them dive-bombed the house. A murder of magpies. She shivered as she recollected their collective name. One of them must be trapped in the attic and causing the noise.

An hour later, in the living-room, with Penny snoozing on her lap, and just as she had started to calm down, she heard Maurice's brand-new Ford Anglia on the gravel drive.

'You're home early. Did you enjoy the golf?' She held out her chin for Maurice's perfunctory kiss.

'Caught you out, haven't I?' He pointed to the tell-tale tumbler. Ice cubes from their new refrigerator bobbed in the gin and tonic. 'Bit early even for you, Carole?'

'I got a fright, Maurice. It's the noises...'

'Did you take your tablets?'

She nodded.

'You shouldn't mix them with alcohol.'

'But Maurice, the noises were loud today. They went on for ages. I'm sure a bird is trapped in the attic.'

He put his hands on his hips. She noticed his trousers were straining around his girth. For someone who claimed to play 18 holes, three times a week, he didn't seem especially fit.

'You're hearing things!'

'You're home early so please check it today.'

Maurice sighed.

'I suppose it could be a trapped bird...' He seemed to notice Penny for the first time. 'How are you, honeybun?'

He nipped her plump cheek between two fingers. Clicked his tongue, winked at her.

27

Penny snuggled further into Carole's arms. With her thumb in her mouth, she stared at her father through china-blue eyes.

'Must call the office.'

She heard his study door slam.

She wondered why he had to call the office on a Sunday. She thought about Rita, his auburn-waved secretary, voluptuous in her tight pencil skirt. She had met Rita at the Christmas dance. The secretary had cast shifty-eyed glances at Carole all night.

She bent her head, enjoying the sweet scent of Penny's hair. Penny wriggled around to face her.

'Daddy's naughty, isn't he?'

'What do you mean?'

'With that lady who was here. He's been naughty.'

Carole remembered that last Saturday she had helped at the church jumble sale.

'What did the lady look like?'

'She had red hair and a big bottom.' Giggling, Penny covered her mouth with her hand.

'What were they doing?'

'They were in daddy's study, playing horses. I was upstairs with my dollies.'

Carole was surprised at the sudden moistness in her eyes. She knew what little love she and Maurice shared had died long ago. But this was monstrous. He had brought his strumpet here, to their house.

'Don't cry, Mummy. You're a good girl. Daddy's naughty.'

Carole took a sip of her drink. The ice had melted. The outside of the glass was slick with condensation. She shivered as the gin hit the spot. It coursed through her veins, warming her. Through the swirling fug in her head, she wondered if Maurice had been plotting with Rita. If the noises were an attempt to drive her mad.

Penny grew heavy in her arms. Carole felt herself dozing.

'Mummy!' Carole was being shaken awake. 'Daddy's shouting.'

'Help me into the attic.' Maurice loomed in the doorway.

Carole stood, brushing the creases from her dress, stifling a yawn. Penny scampered up the stairs ahead. Maurice had brought the step ladder in from the garage.

'You take the bottom of the ladder. I'll take the top.'

Crab-like they inched upstairs.

'Careful!' Maurice yelled as the ladder nicked the wallpaper.

'Hold the ladder tight. It's a bit sticky.'

While Maurice heaved the hatch, Carole watched his stomach straining against his clothes. With a final shove, the hatch flew open. A button popped off his shirt.

He hauled himself into the attic. For a moment, Carole wallowed in a gleeful notion of shutting the hatch, removing the ladder. She wondered how long it would take him to die. If she could stand the racket as he expired.

'Mummy, come and look at my dollies.' Penny tugged her arm.

'Just a minute.'

She heard a shout from overhead.

'There *is* a bird up here!'

'Mummy, come on!' Penny screeched.

'Penny, wait!'

Carole heard Maurice clapping his hands, the panicked fluttering of wings.

'Got it. I'll wring its neck.'

Squawking.

Silence.

'Mummy!' A loud clatter from Penny's room.

As she turned to look at Penny, she took her hands off the ladder. At that moment Maurice descended, one hand holding the dead magpie. As he stepped from the ladder, he lost his footing just as the marbles streamed from Penny's room onto the landing.

It was almost comical. Just like a cartoon. Maurice stumbled. His slippered-feet rolled on the marbles. His arms flailed as he sought to steady himself. Losing his balance, he swallow-dived down the stairs like a gigantic albatross. He crashed into the grandfather clock. His body looked broken, as if every bone had been fractured. A shard of wood through his heart finished him.

Stunned, Carole glanced at Penny. Her baby stood on the landing, thumb in mouth, teddy under arm, china-blue eyes wide with big-girl knowing.

'He was a very naughty boy, Mummy.'

Clare's Fear

Maggie Farran

Clare rushed back into her flat and sat down on her sofa. Her heart was beating so fast she felt as though she would have a heart attack any minute. She was breathing as if she had run a marathon instead of walking along the corridor to the stairs of her block of flats.

'Take a deep breath. Make yourself a cup of tea and you'll feel better,' she muttered to herself.

She drank her tea. Gradually her heart and breathing slowed. She sighed deeply and looked out of her window at Chandler's Ford spread out below her. She had once enjoyed the busy little town. She had loved shopping in Waitrose, having her free coffee, walking round the Lakes, and sitting in the pub garden at the King Rufus. Now all she could do was look at the scene below her and remember the good times she had taken for granted.

She was a prisoner in her own home.

The lovely flat that she had moved into two years ago might as well have been a jail. She'd loved her beautiful house in Hiltingbury Road, but when Jim had died it had seemed sensible to downsize.

The telephone rang in its own cheerful way.

'Hello, Mum, I'm at Asda. What would you like me to get you?'

'Oh, the usual, Sally, I don't want to be any trouble.'

'OK, Mum, I'll be around about four. How is your broken rib?'

'Still a bit painful, but it's getting better.'

Clare went into the kitchen to make herself another cup of tea. She tried to read her book but she couldn't concentrate. She was bored stiff. If only she could go out. She felt like she would go mad if she stayed in for a moment longer.

Three weeks ago, she had been walking through Hiltingbury Park on a lovely warm spring evening. As she bent down to admire the bright yellow daffodils, someone grabbed her handbag. She held onto her bag and shouted loudly for help. The thief knocked her down and kicked her until she let the bag go.

Physically, she had almost recovered. Her bruises had faded. Her rib was a lot less painful. But she felt as vulnerable as ever. Every day she would remember the terror of the attack. She had felt so weak and defenceless.

She had never missed Jim so much as she did now.

The front door opened and Sally let herself in. Clare's spirits lifted at the sight of her daughter.

'Hello, Mum. I'll put your shopping away. You're looking a lot better. You won't need me soon. You'll be able to get your own bits and pieces.'

'Thanks, love. I don't know what I would have done without you. You've been an absolute treasure since the mugging. I think it will be another week or two before I'm recovered enough to go out on my own though.'

Sally gave her one of her serious looks. 'You're not scared are you, Mum? I could understand if you were. It was such a terrifying thing that happened, but the police have got him now. He can't hurt you again.'

'No, it's not that. I just don't feel as if my rib is recovered enough yet.'

Clare hated lying to her daughter but it was such a difficult thing to admit. She had always been so strong and independent. She had been the one to help Sally. Now it was the other way round.

'I'm sorry, love. I hate being needy. I'm only seventy-five, but at the moment I feel twenty years older.'

Sally kissed the top of her head. 'You've done so much for me. It's about time I did something for you. You'll soon feel more like your old self. You've managed so well on your own since Dad died. It can't have been easy.'

Clare gave a little nod and squeezed her daughter's hand.

After Sally had gone Clare rang her best friend, Elizabeth.

'Elizabeth, I don't know what to do. I'm frightened even to get into the lift or go down the stairs since the mugging. I haven't told anyone except you. I feel such a fool. I know I shouldn't really be scared. It's highly unlikely I'll get mugged again. I just don't seem able to control my fear.'

'I'll come round tomorrow morning and we can go to the shops together. You'll feel better having someone with you.'

The next morning, Elizabeth arrived promptly and they had a cup of tea together before they attempted the outing.

'I feel so nervous, Elizabeth, even with you for company.'

'We'll take it slowly. I won't rush you. We'll go to Waitrose for a bit of lunch. You'll be fine with me. I won't put any pressure on you.'

With Elizabeth's support, Clare got out of the flat and into the lift without any problems. Already in the lift was her neighbour, Zoe, with her toddler, Paul, and the baby in a double buggy.

Clare bent down to talk to Paul, trying not to wince at the pain in her rib.

'Hello, darling, aren't you getting a grownup boy now?'

Zoe smiled. 'He's going to be two next week. The time has flown by. Louise is five months already.'

'Louise is such a pretty name,' said Elizabeth as she stroked the baby's chubby cheek.

The ten minute walk to Waitrose was made easier by Elizabeth's kindly chatter. When she was with her best friend Clare felt safe and was able to enjoy her cappuccino and chicken wrap.

'Thanks, Elizabeth. It's so lovely to get out and mix with people again. I know it's silly being too scared to go out on my own. The mugging took away my confidence'

'You don't have to thank me. I know you'd do the same for me. Anyway, I enjoy your company. I've missed our little outings. You should have told me before how scared you were.'

'It's not an easy thing to admit.'

The following day, Clare looked out of her window at the spring sunshine. She decided she was brave enough to go out on her own. She put on her cheerful red coat and her butterfly scarf. She locked the door of her flat.

By the time she reached the lift, her heart was thumping. She was shaking all over. She hurried back to the safety of her flat. She looked out of her window and started to cry.

'I thought I was all over this silliness yesterday. Now I'm back to square one. I need to be able to go out on my own! Now I'm even talking to myself.'

She was staring at the communal garden below when she saw little Paul running across the grass on his own. He was heading towards the main road. She froze.

Zoe lived on the floor above, but she didn't know which flat. There was no time to waste looking for her. She would have to leave the flat on her own. She opened the door with sweaty hands. Her heart thumped against her sore rib. She hurried down the corridor holding onto the wall to steady herself.

She didn't have time to wait for the lift. Gingerly she started to walk down the stairs, holding the handrail. She felt dizzy and sick, but she couldn't turn back now. Through the window she spotted Paul by the road. He had stopped to pick up a discarded ball.

At the main door, she froze again, like a statue. She couldn't seem to make her legs work. She took a breath.

Paul dropped the ball. It rolled into the road. New strength flooded into her. She ran to Paul and seized his hand.

'Paul, sweetheart, we need to find your Mummy. You shouldn't be out on your own.'

She gently led the toddler across the grass towards the entrance to the flats. Just as she got there she saw a frantic-looking Zoe rushing down the stairs, clutching the baby.

'Oh, thank goodness. I was feeding Louise. I didn't notice him leave. I thought he was in his bedroom playing with his toy car. He used a chair to climb up and open the front door. I didn't think he could do that.'

Elizabeth handed Paul back to his relieved mum. Her thoughts returned to herself. She didn't feel scared. Not now. Her heart was only beating fast from running. In fact, she felt marvellous.

'Don't worry, dear. It was nothing. I just happened to be looking out of the window when I saw him. I didn't know I could run so fast myself.'

Clare laughed. The sun was out and the cheerful purple tulips smiled at her from the flower beds. Life in Chandler's Ford was going to be good again.

A Day at the Races

Sally Howard

Hampshire Independent 1883

The October Steeplechase, the fourth meeting of the newly established Chandlers Ford races, is set to be a splendid and colourful spectacle. Our very own race meeting will be sport of the highest character. A first class afternoon's entertainment with respectable company is to be enjoyed by all!

'Girls only ride side-saddle. You'll never win a race, let alone the Chandler's Ford Steeplechase.'

Tears sprang to Georgina's eyes. She turned away from Joe, bowing her head. The curry comb she had been using to groom the bay mare had fallen to the hay-strewn stable floor. She picked it up and worked it in a circular motion down the mare's flank, loosening mud and easing the tension in the taut muscles. The short reddish-brown hair shone with a lustrous sheen in the light filtering through the stable doors.

Her own arms ached, but in a good way. They'd raced the horses through Ramalley Copse, the red-tinged leaves of the wild cherry trees flicking against her bare arms as they had followed the well-worn path through the woods. Joe had won, of course, on Fox Hunter, the big chestnut colt, but she and Lady had caught him on the downhill towards Monks Brook. Under the ancient oaks, they'd let the horses cool and have their head, before heading back to the big house.

She turned back to Joe, who was leaning against a mounting block, watching her, chewing a piece of straw.

'I can ride astride. I've been practising.'

'Even so, how can you enter? You're a girl... and you need a horse.'

Georgina lowered her eyes, focusing on a strand of straw which she worried with her boot.

'Perhaps... I could borrow Lady.'

Joe's eyes widened. 'My mother would never allow it.'

'Just this once? Is it any different than when we take Lady and Fox Hunter out together? We're practically racing the horses. And 50 sovereigns. Think of that! That would mean so much to me to use, for Ma.'

Joe jumped off the mounting block, made to reach for her hand. 'How about —'

A bellow roared from the stable entrance. 'Georgina! Where the devil is that girl?'

Heat ran up Georgina's back. She looked towards the stable doors. The light was fading. She should have finished up here ages ago. Now she'd kept Da waiting.

Joe stepped away from the stall, not exactly hiding, but out of the way. Georgina's father stormed round the edge of the stall. His red-veined cheeks were bright and angry.

'Where are you, girl?' Spittle flew from his mouth. He spotted Joe and pulled up short, touching his cap. 'Master Joe, didn't see you there.'

Joe nodded. 'Evening, Mr Harris.'

Her father turned to Georgina, lowering his shoulders in a visible effort to calm himself.

'As soon as you're finished here, you're needed in the tack room.'

'Yes, Da.'

Her father turned and left. Georgina closed her eyes, breathing deeply to try to control the wave of heat that raced up her face. Da might be an excellent groom, but his temper had not improved of late.

She heard Joe behind her. He stood with a rueful grimace on his face.

'Mother will be expecting me back.'

Georgina nodded. He shouldn't really be here. Lady Hargreave was a stickler for punctuality even if it was just her and her son to supper. She watched him retreat, noticing how his shoulders had widened over the summer.

She realised Joe had paused and was looking at her, an expression she couldn't fathom on his face.

'Can you find time for a ride again tomorrow?' he said.

She smiled. 'Goodnight, Joe.'

That night Georgina lay awake on her bed, tucked up under the eaves of the thatched roof.

A spindly spider wove a web in a corner. Earlier, she'd also noticed a fat-legged house spider scurrying across the flagstones towards the dry warmth of the fire. A sure sign of rain to come.

She twisted her hair round her fingers, long glossy locks which she was somewhat proud of. Not vain. Indeed, she gave her hair the same attention as the mare's mane. There was no harm to it.

A soft moan came from the other bed chamber. Through the thin distempered walls, she heard the creak of wooden struts and crackle of straw-stuffed mattress. Her Ma shifting, unable to get comfortable.

Ma was noticeably worse, the coughing fits longer and deeper, since the first chill of autumn had turned the leaves to gold and bronze. How would she be with the onset of winter snows?

At least Da was out, even if he was in his cups at the New Hut Inn. She sighed. He seemed so much, well, angrier at the world. Her mind followed a well-worn pattern of thought. She knew it was up to her, that she must be the one to keep the family going and help her mother.

The Chandlers Ford Steeplechase was a week away and Lady Hargreave had generously put up a £50 prize. Enough to pay for Ma to visit the sanatorium. Even to stay all winter.

How would she enter the race without a horse? How could she afford the entrance fee? She kicked her blanket in frustration.

The spider spun its silky thread, creating beauty out of nothing. She retrieved her blanket from the floor, pulling it round her ears. She had an idea.

The day of the race dawned grey but fine. The heavy rain clouds of the last few days had cleared with a day's grace to dry out the ground. The going would be heavy; the low-lying ground of the race course would be boggy from the recent rains. But it was Lady's home territory. She would make light work of it, Georgina was sure.

Beside her, Lady snickered, her hoof stamping on the grass that was littered with decaying oak leaves and browning acorns.

'Patience, Lady, patience.' Georgina patted her neck.

In her pocket she felt the weight of a pouch of coins — the entrance fee for the race. Early this morning, she'd sat in Mr Jenson's, the wig makers in Eastleigh, straight-backed and silent. His wife had worked the clippers through her hair like she was shearing a sheep. Not unkindly, she had styled her hair round her face. Georgina ran her hand through the bristles on her neck, unused to the feeling of lightness. Well, never mind. She pulled her cap down tight.

She'd kept out of sight during the preparations for the race. She'd watched from afar as Joe's horse had been groomed and saddled. Joe was resplendent in the navy blue and yellow silks of the house, looking every inch the young country gentleman. The kitchen maids waved as Joe departed.

Once they'd gone, Georgina sneaked into the empty stables. Her fingers shook as she saddled and bridled Lady. Leading her across the courtyard to the woods, she retrieved a bundle of clothes which she'd hidden under a tree -- an old checked shirt and brown corduroy trousers of Da's. Sewing was not her strong point, but she'd made a tolerable job of altering the clothes to fit her.

Now, before her, crowds milled about the race stalls. Bunting flapped in the breeze. Children scampered about with sticky pink cotton-candy faces. The rich aroma of meat pies drifted her way. Round the betting stall, punters shouted, money clasped in clenched fists, trying to catch the attention of the bookmaker, who wore a flamboyant checked suit and bowler hat.

She spotted Joe in the spacious fenced-in paddock. His blue and yellow silks were unmistakeable. Was he wondering where she was? Why she was not there to cheer him on?

She put her hand out to rub Lady's nose, as much to calm herself as to steady her horse. She looked into Lady's eye.

'Time to go.'

She swung astride the saddle. With careful attention, she adopted the easy posture of Joe. She'd been watching him on their rides.

Dismounting, she approached the entrance stall. She laid the money pouch on the table.

The shiny bald head of the clerk remained bent over his ink-spotted ledger. 'Name?'

'George Smith.' She pitched her voice low and cleared her throat, in the manner of one of the farm hands whose voice was breaking.

'Horse?'

'Lady. A bay mare, four years old.'

The small fat fingers of the clerk counted her money then pushed a tattered racing bib towards her.

'Fix that to you. You're number nine. We want a good clean race. No jostling, striking, biting, pushing or other some such cheating.' He grunted. 'Them's the rules. Break 'em and you're out.'

He wrote her number on a betting skip. 'Give this to the bookmaker yonder. Don't bother going to the paddock. We'll be starting soon.'

He rattled the lid down on the money box and began to shut up shop.

She picked up the bib and betting slip and let out a breath. Her heart stopped trying to jump out of her chest. That wasn't so bad. He hadn't even looked up.

She was equally lucky at the betting stall. Her number was chalked up, causing a flurry of renewed activity from the betting fraternity.

A shrill whistle sounded, calling competitors to the starting post — country gentry who possessed a horse of pedigree, and farmhands trying their luck on sturdy work horses cheered on by their white-pinafored sweethearts.

Georgina pushed her way to the starting line, keeping away from Joe, head down, avoiding eye contact. Horses jostled around her. A rider cursed. Her pulse rushed in her ears. Lady pulled beneath her, sensing the excitement. She ran her hands down her neck.

'Not long now.'

The Starter raised his red flag. An audacious rider on a large grey stallion let his horse go and jumped forward. The Starter kept his flag raised, glaring at the defiant jockey. With narrowed eyes, the rider dug in his spurs and wheeled into line again.

Georgina tensed her arms. The flag fell. Lady sprung forward with the other horses.

Galloping down the first stretch mid-field, she calmed her breathing and settled into a rhythm. She calculated the course.

Over the higher ground south of Knight Wood, turn past the station — careful of the boggy ground — then the home stretch to the grand stand. One circuit, 1 and 1/4 miles. Manageable. Just stay on course.

Tightly packed, the horses approached the water jump. Mud splattered in her face. Lady rose, then slammed back to earth with a jar. They were over.

Air rushed past her ears. Trees flashed in a green blur. Hooves thumped on the rough grass. She guided Lady up through the field, farm horses and inexperienced riders falling behind.

Joe was ahead in the front pack, adopting the new 'American seat' — head down, knees up. The big grey stallion, the defiant jockey abusing his horse with whip and spur, came dangerously close, nearly touching Joe's foot and putting him off his stride. Joe turned his head. Clearly not liking what he saw, he pulled Fox Hunter's head round.

Georgina drew alongside. Joe glanced her way, his eyes widening as he saw Lady and even wider when he recognised her. She couldn't help but smile and was gratified when he grinned back.

The grey stallion was ahead of them, but losing pace, the rider rolling in the saddle as he spurred on his horse. He came level with Joe, veered towards him and cannoned his great brute of a horse into Fox Hunter's flank. Fox Hunter stumbled. Joe pulled at the reins. He slipped to the side of his saddle.

Georgina cried out. She saw Joe fall, tuck himself into a roll and scramble out of the way of the remaining riders. Oh, thank goodness he was safe!

She gritted her teeth and bent low over Lady's neck. It was just her and the grey stallion now. They rode neck and neck, thundering down the straight to the finish line. Lady's ears were down. She was giving it her all.

Georgina blinked wind-tears from her eyes. She could see the finish post, the raised flag ready to fall.

'Come on, Lady. You can do it.'

Lady sensed she was near the finish. Georgina felt her stride lengthen. They edged in front of the grey stallion. The rider flourished his whip. Spit flew from the stallion's mouth as it veered towards them. It pushed into Lady's side, edging her to the wrong side of the finish post. Georgina tugged at the reins. Lady's head came round — she saw the muscles straining down her neck — but the grey stallion was too big. Lady couldn't resist him. She couldn't ask it of her. She yielded.

The grey stallion thundered across the line. The flag came down.

They had lost.

Georgina leaned her face against Lady's neck. She was in the paddock, rubbing down Lady with a brush she had borrowed from one of the grooms. She felt drained, empty. It had all been for nothing. Beaten by a cheat.

A cheering crowd surrounded the winning stallion. The rider, a singular fellow -- tall, well-attired in grey silks -- made his way to the winner's enclosure. He tipped his hat at her in a most impertinent manner. She looked away, stomach churning.

Where was Joe? There was no sign of him. Her heart beat loudly in her ears. He wasn't hurt, was he?

The winner was escorted to the trophy platform in front of the grandstand, a rough structure of wooden planking. Lady Hargreave, resplendent in a forest-green riding habit, stood beside a draped table with a plate and bag of coins. She held out her gloved hand and the gentleman — no, he was no gentleman — stepped forward to receive the plate and prize money.

Georgina was about to turn away — she couldn't watch any longer — when a disturbance parted the crowd. Joe was striding to the platform, a steward at his side. He beckoned to the Clerk of the Course, a short fellow in a sombre grey suit, and whispered at length in his ear. The Clerk nodded and straightened. He cleared his throat. The crowd hushed.

'There has been a complaint of foul riding.'

A shiver ran through the crowd.

The winner narrowed his eyes. He raised his hand in a broad, sweeping gesture.

'I am at a loss to understand any point on which a dispute can be made.'

The Clerk blinked rapidly, pushing thin spectacles up his nose. 'The dispute, sir, is that you did purposefully and with intent, jostle Mr Hargreave here, on the horse Fox Hunter, unseating him, and thereafter, jostled the second place horse, in the same manner, thereby allowing for your own winning in a most unsportsmanlike manner.'

The winner tapped his whip on the side of his leather boots. 'A false accusation, sir. Tired horses bump into each other all the time.'

'Mr Gregor, the Finish Line Steward, upholds the claim, sir. And consequently —'

'He's a liar.'

The gentleman clenched his fist and stepped forward. The Clerk shrunk backwards, then recollecting the number of witnesses at his back, regained his composure.

'You are disqualified, sir.'

The gentleman raised himself to his full height. Glancing at the crowd, he seemed to think better of any further show of force.

'Confound you!' he shouted, and stormed off.

The Clerk shook himself like a dog shaking off an annoying fly. He consulted his little book.

'Consequently the winner is... George Smith, on the horse Lady.' His eyes searched the crowd. 'Where is George Smith?'

Georgina stood frozen to the spot. She couldn't believe her ears. Had that really happened? The cheat had been found out? Justice had prevailed?

On the other side of the crowd, Joe was grinning at her.

She stepped forward. The crowd turned, parted for her. An over-eager bystander thumped her on the back. 'Well done, lad.'

Her cap fell to the ground.

Someone shouted. 'Why, it's a girl!'

The chant was taken up by the crowd.

'Not right and proper!' said a portly woman to Georgina's right.

There was Mr Hodges, the postman, and other townspeople whom she knew, all staring at her. She wanted to shrink into her skin.

The Clerk had his head together with his deputy, consulting a faded brown rule book. He held up his hands for quiet.

'There's nothing says a lass can't race.'

There were murmurs in the crowd and someone wolf-whistled. Georgina held her breath.

'Not unless it is a fraudulent entry or running under a false description.' He turned to Georgina. 'Is this horse in fact called Lady as you presented her?'

Everyone was staring at her. Georgina's mouth was dry. She licked her lips.

'Yes, she is Lady.'

'And are you qualified to enter her?'

Georgina hesitated. She could feel sweat trickling down her back. Did she have permission to enter Lady in the race? No. She didn't think of it as *stealing* Lady Hargreave's horse, just *borrowing* her for the race. Of course, she was going to ride her back to the stable afterwards. But how would it appear?

'Er...' She didn't know how to go on. She stood there, blinking, a mouse caught in a trap.

A shout came from the crowd.

'Let her 'ave it.' It was her Da. He stepped out from the onlookers and gestured with his hands. 'She's a good girl, she is.'

He grabbed her hand and shook it vigorously. Georgina was stunned. She stood still while he pumped her hand up and down.

'Well done, lass,' he whispered. 'You did it for yer Ma, didn't you?'

The Clerk ignored this exchange. 'I must have an answer. Who owns this horse?'

A hush fell.

'I own the horse,' Lady Hargreave said.

The crowd sighed.

The Clerk turned to her, with a small bow of the head. 'Did you give permission for the horse to enter the race?'

Joe jumped onto the platform. 'I gave permission.'

Lady Hargreave raised her eyebrows at him. The Clerk looked at her. Eventually she nodded.

'Lady wins the race!' He slammed the rule book shut. 'No further discussion will be entered into. The decision of the Clerk is final.'

The crowd roared. Georgina thought her heart would burst.

Joe was in animated conversation with his mother, Lady Hargreave. He glanced at Georgina several times.

Georgina stood motionless on the platform, gripping the plate and bag of money to her chest. The crowd had dispersed, leaving only the wind to whip discarded betting slips round the empty enclosure. Her mind whirled over the ups and downs of the day.

Joe came over.

'Well done,' he said. He adopted a faint air of reproach on his face. 'You could have told me, you know. Trusted me.'

She hung her head. 'I'm sorr...' Her voice broke.

The day's emotions swept over her. She felt weak at the knees, her energy spent. She sat down on the edge of the platform, staring at, but not seeing, the odd job man as he pulled down the bunting.

Joe sat down beside her.

'I'm sorry,' she said. 'I didn't want to get you into trouble.' She looked up at him. 'Thank you, Joe.' The words felt insufficient.

He didn't say anything for a time. Her heart sank. Was he really so angry with her? She may have won the money for her Ma — and that was important to her — but she had lost a good friend in the process.

Eventually she asked. 'Is your mother so very angry?'

He chuckled. 'No, not really. I talked her round. Besides she likes you.'

Georgina frowned at him. 'She likes me?'

He ventured nothing further. Georgina sat in miserable contemplation, replaying in her head the better plan of asking for his help, rather than embarking on her own hare-brained scheme.

She couldn't understand the expression on his face, but it seemed there was nothing more to be said. With a sigh, she stood up to leave. He grabbed her fingers, pulling her down towards him.

'So,' he said, and cleared his throat.

He ran his fingers through the short hair of her fringe.

'So, next time ...'

History: Horse racing took place in Chandler's Ford between 1883 – 1885, with several meetings taking place each year. The probable location of the race course is to the west of Chandler's Ford station, the current location of Shannon Way, Wicklow Drive and Foyle Road.

The going was indeed 'heavy and treacherous', despite efforts to drain and level the course. Nevertheless, it was well attended, at its height attracting "a veritable galaxy of nobility and gentry', the Railway offering an 'enhanced train service for race goers" and such entertainment as 'itinerant minstrels, cheapjacks, travelling shows, shooting galleries, a bowling alley and even performing monkeys'.

Racing ceased in 1885, in part due to changes to Jockey Club rules. Fumes from the rapidly developing brickyards and kilns to the east of the course, on the site of today's Industrial Estate, may also have been a discouragement for race-goers.

Many thanks to Eastleigh Museum for their kind assistance.

George and the Dragon

Catherine Griffin

George loitered over the sandwiches. It was Tuesday. He normally bought chicken salad on a Tuesday, juice, and maybe a bag of crisps if he felt like it. But there was a whole world of sandwiches to choose from. Maybe he should try something different. Would she notice if he bought smoked salmon?

His heart beat faster at the thought of her, of her soft questioning eyes lifted to his as she scanned his sandwich. Maria. His reason for being here.

Here in Asda, buying lunch, that was.

He checked his watch and realised he'd been staring at sandwiches for ten minutes. Only half his lunch hour remained. He compromised by snatching a premium chicken sandwich, then headed for the check-outs.

As always, his chest tightened and his heart raced. Would she be there? Would she recognize him? Would she say something, or would he try to say something to her and stumble over his words, and then would she laugh, or coldly ignore him?

But there she was, at her usual checkout. The same as yesterday and every day for the last two weeks. Dark hair shining under the fluorescent lights, soft dark eyes gazing at nothing as she waited for the next customer. Waiting for him. His mouth went dry. Anxiety coiled round his throat.

He placed the sandwich and drink on her conveyor with exaggerated care, intensely aware of his awkward tallness and the stubborn extra pounds around his middle. His items slid towards her. He had to lift his head and meet her eyes. Her eyes, oh, her eyes that he wanted to drown in, and her smile.

'Huh, hullo.' She had a name badge, though he didn't need to look at it. Her name was written on his soul. 'Maria. Huh, how are you today?'

He adjusted his own badge, the security badge from work which he normally took off, but today he hoped she would notice his name.

She passed him his sandwich and his bottle of juice.

'Kesh or kart?' she said.

'Kesh. I mean, cash.'

He counted out the exact change. The passing warmth of her hand was electric. He thought she lingered a fraction longer than yesterday, that her smile was warmer. Perhaps it was only his imagination. He tore himself away and walked fast to the exit before he looked back. She was dealing with another customer.

There was a bench in the car park where he liked to sit and eat his sandwich. He watched the cars come and go in the sunshine, the way the shadow of the trees moved in the breeze. Enjoyed the fresh air scented with exhaust fumes and the sparrows chirping. But mostly, he thought about Maria.

He loved her. He thought she knew, that his unasked questions met a silent answer in her eyes and her smile. But she never said anything. Was she waiting for him to speak first?

He wanted to but when he tried to speak he felt that cold grip on his throat, choking back the words, and the doubts flooded in. He would only stutter, and she would laugh. How could she ever take seriously a stupid lump like himself, still living with his mother at 24, dumped by every girlfriend he'd ever had (not that there had been many)?

What if that wasn't the problem though? He chewed thoughtfully. She had an accent. Eastern European, he thought. Maybe she didn't speak much English.

He threw his sandwich crust to a pigeon, then got his phone out of his pocket. With the internet at hand, language was no problem. Which language though? Maybe she was Polish. Maria could be a Polish name.

It might be a bit soon to say 'I love you'. Perhaps something simple like, 'Hello. I'm George. Would you go out with me?'

He tapped 'Hello' into Google Translate, then listened to the Polish translation.

'Chesh,' he said to the pigeon. It looked unimpressed.

'Yestem George.' The bird waddled off. 'Sesh eesh ze noh?'

Polish had a lot of funny accented characters and hardly any vowels. The odd thing was, as he struggled to pronounce the strange words, he realised he wasn't stuttering at all.

The time displayed on his phone brought him back to the present. Time to go back to work. Another exciting afternoon of checking badges. He brushed the crumbs from his uniform and dropped the remains of his lunch in the bin, still mouthing Polish phrases to himself.

Wednesday was usually cheese, but in a rush of euphoria, he picked the smoked salmon instead. He wasn't even sure he liked smoked salmon. That wasn't important though. He'd been up half the night memorising handy Polish phrases and he was determined he wasn't going to wimp out. Today was the day he would talk to Maria.

There was someone ahead of him at her check-out, an old lady fumbling with coupons. She smelt of tobacco and cats. The girl on the next till waved him over, and he smiled his apology. Finally the old lady finished cramming tins of tuna into her old-lady-caddy, and it was his turn.

He took a deep breath, stared into Maria's eyes, and rattled out 'Hello, Maria. My name is George. How are you today?' in his best internet Polish.

She blinked in surprise. He held his breath.

'Zorry,' she said. 'Kesh or kart?'

'Cash.' He handed over a ten pound note in such a state of shock, he hardly noticed her fingers brushing his when she handed back the change.

Carrying his lunch, he walked out of the shop, still numb. She hadn't understood. Had his Polish been wrong? Did she just pretend not to understand? Or maybe....

He stopped and was nearly run over by a speeding Volvo.

Maybe she wasn't Polish. He'd only guessed she was Polish. There were lots of countries in Eastern Europe though. He couldn't try all the languages until he hit on the right one. Well, he could, but it would be better not to. He needed to know where she was from.

He returned to work and told his manager he was sick. It was hardly pretence; the smoked salmon had made him a bit queasy. Ten minutes moping convinced his boss to release him for the rest of the day.

George went back to his usual seat in the car park, and watched.

He wasn't sure what he was doing or why, only that he had to know more about Maria. Maybe he really was ill. He felt feverish. Guilty too, for lying to his boss, and for spying on Maria. He felt like a stalker. Of course, he was stalking her, but he didn't see what else he could do.

Around 3 o'clock, he saw her come out. He would recognize her trim dark figure anywhere, even if it was only a glimpse. She came out of the front doors, walked across the car park and up the ramp to the bus stop where she waited, looking at her phone.

George trotted across the car park. Maybe he could follow her home, or at least see what bus she got on. Before he got there, a car pulled up. A battered red Nissan, driven by a shaven-headed young man. Maria opened the car door and got in. The man spoke to her, she replied, then the car sped off in a pall of black diesel fumes.

He watched them go, unable to take his eyes from the scene as all his pitiful hopes and dreams crashed around him.

She had a boyfriend. Or a husband, although he'd checked her hands were free of rings. It must be a boyfriend and that was bad enough. Probably he had cheekbones and piercing blue eyes. If nothing else, he at least spoke her language.

George didn't have a chance.

His mother thought he was ill. She fussed over him and he let her, but didn't tell her why he was pale and miserable and refused second helpings of lasagne. He made sandwiches at home to take to work with him, though he didn't think he'd eat them. His manager thought he'd had food poisoning and didn't object to his being late.

He slouched through the day, replying in mutters to his co-workers when they tried to cheer him up. Though the sun shone, he felt his life had ended in that one moment of agony. To shut Maria from his mind and heart was impossible. The best he could hope for was that the pain would dull in time, so he could go through the motions of life again and pretend nothing was wrong.

Displaying a kindness as unexpected as it was unprecedented, his manager sent him home early.

'Get a good night's sleep, lad. You'll feel better tomorrow.'

George wanted to say he would never feel better, that he was only a hollow shell of a man forever more, but he just thanked him and left.

His route home took him to past Asda and the bus stop. He walked slowly, cringing inside at the possibility of seeing her again, but when he saw her waiting at the bus stop there was only dull shock. She raised her head from her phone and looked straight at him as he stood frozen on the other side of the road.

She smiled at him as if she remembered his face, and his heart stopped. What would he have given, two days ago, for her to recognize him and smile.

In a waft of diesel, the red Nissan pulled up at the bus stop, dividing them. George stared at his nemesis, registering the shaved-head, chiselled jaw-line, and tattooed arm.

Maria bent down to the open car window. She said a few words, shaking her head. The man gestured and shouted something. She backed away from the car. The driver flung open his door and got out, speaking loudly and continuously in a language George didn't recognize. He rounded the car and grabbed Maria's arm. She twisted, trying to get away. George saw her grimace in pain.

Before he could think, without even looking both ways, he crossed the road.

'Excuse me,' he said.

The man did indeed have cheekbones and piercing blue eyes which met George's gaze levelly. A short-sleeved T-shirt showed off the serpent tattoos snaking round corded muscle. George glanced at Maria.

He couldn't claim to be brave. Yes, he was nominally a security guard, but he never had to do anything except turn up in his uniform. In the event of real trouble he'd call the police like any sensible person. But the fear in Maria's eyes brought out something in him that he had never known was there. For her sake, he would risk anything.

He squared his shoulders and took his badge from his jacket pocket. He held it up, surprised to find his hand wasn't shaking.

'I d-don't think the lady wants to go with you. Let her go or I'll... call the police.'

For a moment, the thug held his ground. George stared back firmly, sure he was about to be beaten to a bloody pulp and left for dead on the pavement. He didn't care. Death was better than a life of hopeless misery.

The man thrust Maria away from him with what sounded like a

curse. She reeled into George's arms. Shaved-head got into the car and drove off with a squeal of tires, leaving only a cloud of black smoke behind him.

George reluctantly released Maria.

'Are you all right? Should I call the police?'

She shook her head. 'No. Is my boyfriend, but no more.' She touched the badge George still held, and smiled. 'Zhank you. George. Like Saint George?'

'Yes, that's it.'

'You save me like Saint George save princess from dragon. You know?'

'Of course. He's the patron saint of England.'

'Is saint my country too. Romania.'

'Really? I didn't know. Your English is very good.'

She blushed. 'Is no good. I learn.'

A bus drew up beside them. He stared into her eyes, transfixed.

'I go bus,' she said.

'Oh. Well, goodbye. Call the police if he gives you any more trouble. And...'

She paused on the step of the bus, looking back at him, her dark eyes soft and inquisitive.

'I'll see you tomorrow?'

She nodded.

The Skating Party

Karen Stephen

'You need to take more care, child!' Marianne winced as Miss Hershey, her governess, dabbed the wound on her knee with iodine. 'You are nearly ten now.'

'The road was icy. I was practising skating with John.' Marianne blinked away tears as blood seeped down her leg.

'There will be no skating.' Miss Hershey stood up.

'But if Hiltingbury Lake freezes...'

'No more nonsense.' Miss Hershey's jet-black skirts swished as she turned towards the library. 'And there's no-one called John!'

Gulping, Marianne sat on the bottom stair pressing a gauze pad onto the cut. Miss Hershey was so unfair.

Marianne wished her father's job with the railway company in Eastleigh did not take him away for such long spells. She was left with Miss Hershey, the grumpy cook and that silly maid who fluttered around gawping at draymen. Thank goodness for John. He'd told her he'd had a governess just like Miss Hershey.

The bleeding stopped. Marianne heard a whistle. *Ring a Ring a Roses*. A tousled-blond head was visible through the dimpled, stained-glass window. John. How could Miss Hershey say he did not exist?

Marianne sprang to the door. John stood on the wide step in plum-coloured velvet breeches and matching cap.

'Poor Marianne, has she been horrible to you again?'

'She's so stupid. She said you don't exist.'

'Well that is stupid, because I'm right here in front of you, talking to you. Aren't I?' He giggled. 'Come on, let's play.'

Marianne paused when she thought of her hurt leg.

'Come *on*!'

Marianne grabbed her coat and muffler.

John skipped. She followed with caution. The ice she had slipped on earlier had melted.

'Let's go to the lake!'

At Hiltingbury Lake, they skimmed stones. Daylight faded. Marianne shivered as it grew colder. She watched with envy as John's willowy arm, his long pale fingers, grasped a stone, angled it, set it skimming five or six times across the water. After yet another of her stones sank with a plonk into the lake, she turned to make a face at John. He was gone.

'John?' She ducked around the reed banks calling for him.

A cackling screech of ravens from the nearby trees the only reply.

At tea-time, Miss Hershey was frosty as usual.

'Your father will be home at the weekend. We shall recite *La Belle Dame Sans Merci* to him. We must also finish the Chopin piece on the piano.'

Marianne's giddy excitement about seeing Father was tempered by the effort expected by Miss Hershey.

She opened her mouth to say something. Catching the glint in Miss Hershey's eye, she swallowed the words.

Snuggled in bed, she cuddled teddy close. The fire in the hearth was dying. The room felt chilly. She would ask Father about skating on the lake if it froze. He would let her do it. She was nearly ten after all.

'Horrid, Horrid Hershey.' A whispering hiss sung to *Ring a Ring o' Roses*.

She sat bolt upright.

'John!' He was sitting on the end of her bed.

He placed a pallid finger to his lips.

'Don't let Horrid, Horrid Hershey hear you.' He smirked.

'Where did you come from?' Her breath pooled into clouds.

'Go to sleep, little one.'

He tucked her into bed, humming all the while.

Next morning, the inside of Marianne's windows was covered with thick jagged whorls of ice. Fascinated, Marianne ran her finger around it, shivering at its delicious coldness.

'Now, Miss, don't be doing that. You'll get frostbitten fingers!' The maid was shovelling coal into the fire. 'You don't want to go near ice, do's you after what happened?'

'Why, what happened?' Something tugged in Marianne's mind. A memory shimmered just beyond reach.

The maid's eyes widened in shock, her hand shot to cover her mouth.

'I shouldn't have said nothing.'

A dark shadow loomed behind her.

'Leave!' Miss Hershey's voice quavered with menace as she pointed at the maid.

63

'What did happen, Miss Hershey? I remember something about the lake and ice.'

'Nothing happened, child. Stop this nonsense and get dressed.'

After lunch, Miss Hershey told her to take some air in the garden. The day had stayed chilly.

The gardener was chipping at the ice in the pond.

'Just making the air hole bigger, Miss. Help the fish to survive.'

As she gazed at the pond, she felt woozy. Something tugged at her memory again. A rush of voices. Skating. Laughter. A hole in the ice. Screaming. She swayed.

'You're bone-frozen, Miss.' The gardener scooped her into his arms.

The trees rustled. She thought she heard the whispering song 'Horrid, Horrid Hershey'.

'John!' she called.

Miss Hershey's pinched face loomed over her.

'There is no John!'

The world went black.

When she woke later, she heard a murmur of voices in the drawing-room. Father! She dashed downstairs.

'I don't want her told!' He sounded angry.

Quivering in her nightgown, Marianne paused outside the wood-panelled door to the drawing-room.

'She keeps mentioning John. I think the memories are surfacing.' Miss Hershey's voice was calm.

'It's better she forgets.'

'I suggest it's better for her to remember. Six years have passed.'

'I want to protect my daughter.'

The maid appeared from the kitchen and hustled Marianne

upstairs.

That night, her dreams came in fragments. A skating party of happy adults in coats, furs, hats. A sweet-faced smiling woman. A glimpse of Father. A rosy-cheeked John. A dark, gaping hole. Ravens squawking against a crimson sky. A black-skirted figure hovering in the distance.

Her scream awoke her.

John was sitting on the end of her bed.

'It's snowing. The lake is frozen now.' He pointed to the window. In the gloom, his cheeks looked grey, his eyes watery-pale. 'Let's skate.'

'I must ask Father.' Her teeth chattered in the frigid air.

'Come...' He hummed *Ring a Ring o'Roses*.

She followed him along the corridor, upstairs to the attic. At times he seemed to vanish into the inky night. Then she'd hear him singing.

He stood by a huge open trunk. She lifted a fur muffler, kid-skin gloves. The scent of mimosa. Mother! In a flash, she remembered what she hadn't realised she had forgotten. She'd had a mother who had died. A deep surge of longing flooded her.

She remembered that they had been skating on Hiltingbury Lake. Giggling, Mother, Marianne, and John had danced to Ring o'Roses. Father was at the far end of the lake with the rest of the party, except for Miss Hershey. She wobbled at the side, refusing to skate any further. They swirled, laughed.

She rifled in the trunk. Her fingers smoothed crushed fabric. She recognised John's plum-coloured breeches and hat. Bemused, she looked around. He had gone again.

She heard singing in the corridor. *Ring a Ring o'Roses*.

John beckoned her downstairs. His cold, thin hand took hold of hers. He dragged her out of the house, along the cobbles, towards the lake.

'Stop, John!' she yelled.

He tightened his bony grip on her, dragging her through the reed beds towards the frozen lake.

'Skate with me, Marianne.'

John heaved her onto the ice. She tried to dig her heels into the ground. He was stronger. Her bare feet were slipping, sliding on the icy lake.

'Ring a Ring o'Roses. Sing, Marianne!'

'Marianne! Come back. Don't go with him.' A sharp voice snapped through her memories.

She turned to the shore. Black-skirts billowed stark against the snowy landscape. Miss Hershey.

John snarled at Miss Hershey, yanking harder on Marianne's arms.

'It's not safe, child! Come back.'

Another lightning flash of memory.

A crack had ripped through the ice. Mother and John stood on a sliver that splintered in savage bursts. Mother's mouth formed an "O" shape. John screamed.

She had cried for Father. Screeched at Miss Hershey to help. Miss Hershey took a few tentative steps, stumbled, fell onto the ice. The ravens circled, cawing.

Marianne sobbed as the memories engulfed her. Her loss felt enormous. John had got it wrong though. Miss Hershey had tried hard to help.

She looked around. John stood in the distance shimmering as if a thousand stars sparkled within him.

A swish of black-skirts.

'There, there, child. I've got you. Thank goodness I made it this time.' Miss Hershey hugged her.

From a distance, Marianne heard John singing *Ring a Ring o'Roses*.

Printer Problems

Sally Howard

'Stupid, stupid printer.'

Megan dropped the instruction leaflet onto her desk, where it fluttered to the floor in a crackle of cheap paper. She glared at the lifeless hunk of plastic on her desk.

'Why won't you print?'

She gathered up her hair where it clung to her neck. Spending a hot and humid Friday evening wrestling with a new printer was not her idea of fun. The printer had seemed such a bargain from the new electrical store grand-opening-extravaganza last Saturday. Now she knew better. She kicked the instructions about the floor until they were thoroughly crumpled.

She picked up the phone to call her dad. He would sort out the problem in no time at all. Her finger hovered over the buttons. Although she knew Dad would still be up, she put the phone back in its cradle.

Leaning back in her chair, she stared at the cold dregs of coffee at the bottom of her mug.

She loved her new flat. The location was ideal. She could walk into Chandler's Ford and meet her friends at Costa's. The train station was just down the road. Perfect.

But she couldn't keep relying on Dad for every small thing that didn't work. Last week he'd fixed the leaking tap in the bathroom. The week before the TV aerial. She needed to stand on her own two feet. That meant she was going to figure this out by herself.

She retrieved the instructions from the floor and smoothed them against her jeans.

'You will be making sure the printer is connected to the wireless,' she read. 'Geez, who writes this stuff? If you told me how to connect it to the wireless it might help.'

She had a strong urge to shout at it.

The setup wizard finally invoked its magic and popped up a list of wireless connections. There were quite a few to choose from: it seemed everyone was on BT Broadband in her block of flats. She chuckled at the one named sparkly-unicorn-donkeys.

Wearily she clicked on the one ending in 'KM'. The printer chirped merrily and a little screen popped up: 'Congratulations, completed printer setup. Welcome to enjoy.'

'OK, that's more like it.' She patted the top of the printer. 'Now let's see if you can print something.'

Grabbing the mouse, she opened a new document, typed in 'hello', and clicked on print. She waited. Nothing happened. Not a sound.

Ding! A little window popped up on the computer: 'Successful is printing.'

'What? No, please don't do this to me!' Nothing had come out the printer. 'Successful is not printing!'

She clicked on print. Again nothing, no sound. No whirring of gears or paper floating neatly into the tray. The little window popped up on the screen again, taunting her with 'Successful is printing.'

'OK, fine. You win!'

Picking up her coffee mug, she headed for the kitchen. A cool breeze blew in through the open window. She could see a light from her neighbour's window — the new guy's flat.

She'd passed him at the bins. He'd been squeezing collapsed boxes into the regular black bin and she'd had to show him where the recyclables went. As he'd lifted his rubbish from one bin to another, she couldn't help gawping at his T-shirt stretched taut across his shoulder muscles. He'd smiled. She'd turned away, face flushing, and had not been able to look at him again.

For a weird moment she wondered whether he was home alone battling with an uncooperative printer too. Now you're being daft, she told herself.

The kettle came to the boil, whistling and bubbling ferociously. While she waited for it to settle, she heaped a spoonful of Kenco Millicano into her Happy Jackson mug.

With a rattle and whir, she heard the printer start up. Grabbing her coffee, she went back into the lounge to see the print heads slide smoothly left to right and a sheet of paper chug into the tray. So now the printer had decided to print her page?

The printer dinged in satisfaction at its first successful print. She pulled the paper out. Across the top, it read: 'hello, how are you?'

A shiver ran up her back and prickled the hairs on her neck. She opened up her document. Yes, she had only typed in 'hello'. How odd. It was almost as if... as if the printer had answered her.

She shook herself. Don't be silly, she thought. She slid the paper back in the in-tray, typed 'I'm fine.' into her document, and printed it.

She took a big gulp of coffee and waited. The little window popped up on the screen: 'Successful is printing.'

The printer sprang into life again. Her heart hammered in her chest, as a piece of paper was pushed out. She picked it up and read: 'Excellent :-) :-).'

Was this some sort of funny welcome program that the printer manufacturer had installed?

Another page chugged out the printer: 'I'm Jack. Nice to meet you.'

Whoa. She stared at the page, her throat gone dry.

The printer remained silent, waiting for her reply. She could only stare at the page blankly.

Another paper chugged out: 'Well, this is fun, but I guess we need to sort this out.'

'How do you want to do that?' she wrote.

'I could pop round.'

'OK. When?'

'Now's as good a time as any.'

'OK. Do you know where I am?'

'Of course!'

Megan sat back in the chair. Her heart pounded in her chest like it was trying to escape. How did whoever-it-was know where she lived?

There was a tap at her door. She opened it to see the new guy standing there. Up close, she could see mahogany eyes beneath artfully messy brown hair. She was in danger of gawping again.

He grinned, then waved a crumpled instruction leaflet very

much like her own.

'Shall we untangle our printers?'

Realisation dawned as he sat at her desk, deftly clicking through the setup wizard with a mastery that was mind-boggling to her.

'See,' he said, 'our wireless names are very similar. You picked mine.' He placed his hand over his heart. 'I take full responsibility. I hadn't gotten round to setting up security after my move. But a doddle to fix.'

'Security?' she said. 'I just know that mine ends with "KM".'

'A foolproof method of selection, I see.'

She put her hand on her hip. 'I'll have you know, it's my favourite coffee. Kenco Millicano.'

'In that case, an excellent choice.' A smile played on his lips. He put his hand on his chin and pretended to stroke it thoughtfully. 'Upon reflection, this may take a while to fix.'

She rolled her eyes. 'Really? Thought you said it was a doddle.'

He grinned sheepishly.

'I guess you'd like a coffee too, while you fix it.'

'Another excellent suggestion.'

Looking for Love

Karen Stephen

Friday, at last. Irene settled into a rattan chair on her patio. She raised her tired, aching legs onto a footstool. The rays of the setting sun bathed her plants in golden hues. Bliss.

'Cooee! Fancy a glass of wine?'

Blinking awake, Irene wiped away a dribble. She sighed. By the gate, her neighbour Joan was waving a bottle of rosé towards her, a hopeful look on her face.

'Come in.'

Joan clip-clopped across the patio in her high-heeled mules.

'Thanks, love. I've fallen out with Dev so thought I'd pop over.'

'Not again!'

'It's a passionate relationship. The best bit is making-up!' Joan cackled.

Irene fought to suppress the unwanted images.

Bottle opened, Joan rifled in her flowery handbag, pulling out a sheaf of papers.

'I've brought some stuff for you about clubs and dating.'

Irene bridled.

'I bet you've not been out all week and you're not going out this weekend either,' Joan retorted.

'I've told you before. I'm fine as I am. I've got my work, the kids, the garden.'

'One of your kids is currently travelling in Vietnam. The other lives in Birmingham.'

'We Skype every week. Why are you on my case?'

'I want you to be happy. Just like me and Dev.'

Irene chortled.

'Well, on a good day that is.'

'Show me what you've got then.'

Irene flicked through flyers for social clubs, speed-dating, singles nights.

'I don't know, Joan… it's all so daunting.'

'I'll come with you the first time.'

'I really don't need a man!'

Later, in the kitchen, as she opened a drawer to put away Joan's bumpf, the handle that she had carefully super-glued last week came away in her hand.

'See? Men do have their uses!' Joan guffawed, swaying a little on the bar stool.

'I can get a handyman to fix that.'

'You can't get handymen for love or money in Chandler's Ford. Better to get the real thing.'

Joan slithered to the floor.

'Time to get you home.' Irene sighed.

Giving her a hug, Joan slurred, 'It's been ten years since Tom died. Time to move on'.

The next day, chores complete, Irene flicked on the TV. Sport or mindless reality shows. The latest Man Booker winner to read. Worthy but dull.

She stood by the patio doors. Smoky barbecue aromas drifted reminding her of past family gatherings. From the surrounding gardens she heard adults talking, laughing. Children playing. All of Valley Park seemed to be having a good time with friends and family. She was alone.

She rested her forehead against the cool glass. Perhaps Joan was right.

A flash of sunlight lit up a silver frame. Her favourite family photo. The four of them on their last holiday. Tom's capable hands rested on the children's shoulders. His kind eyes crinkled with laughter. Behind them the Mediterranean sparkled. She wiped away a tear, remembering his sudden death one month later.

Making a coffee, she flicked through the leaflets. Tonight, Winchester Science Centre was holding a singles night. She felt a painful quiver of excitement. Dare she?

Dialling Joan's number, she shuddered at the voicemail message saying she and Dev were "otherwise engaged."

'You can do this,' she told her reflection in the mirror.

Two hours later, Irene drifted around the fringes of the Science Centre. A hubbub of excited voices echoed in the vast space. She gripped her glass of orange juice. A bespectacled man was heading towards her.

'Hello there. You look as nervous as I feel.'

'Hi, erm, yes... It's the first time I've done this.' She trembled, couldn't even look at him.

'Shall we play with some of the gizmos?'

As he led her towards a complicated plastic structure, he murmured about the weather, the crowd. She liked his woody aftershave. He had a lop-sided, gentle smile. Her heart thudded.

'I'm sorry… I can't do this.'

Irene scuttled to her car.

'Well done for trying,' Joan consoled her later over the phone.

'I'm a bit annoyed that I ran away. He seemed quite nice.'

'Why not try internet dating? You can talk by email before meeting them?'

'I'm not sure…'

'All you need to do is upload a photo and write a bit about yourself.'

During the wet Sunday that followed, Irene scribbled, crossed-out, and rewrote a few lines about herself. She checked her phone for recent photos. In her mind's eye, she was still around 43-ish. Recent selfies reminded her she was nearly 56. Lines etched cobweb-like around her eyes. Cheekbones still good. Chin pouched like a hamster's.

She hauled a box of photos from the dresser. Welling up with tearful nostalgia, she gazed at images of Tom, their wedding day, happy family life.

One photo, from around twelve years ago, showed her sitting on a beach smiling, the wind whipping her hair. She'd always thought she looked a little like Jackie Kennedy in that photo. She would put this photo on the internet. It was her and yet it wasn't. What harm could it do?

The next day, she was astonished to find 8 messages in her inbox. Five of them she deleted immediately. Weirdos. The other three were interesting. Terry from Totton, Clive from Winchester, and Ray from Chandler's Ford.

Time flew as messages pinged back and forth. With giddy excitement, Irene barely took time to eat when she returned home from work. She couldn't wait to open her laptop to read the emails from the hopefuls. The messages grew more flirtatious. Irene hadn't felt like this for years.

The days passed. She started to worry. They all seemed so likeable. What if she couldn't decide between the three of them? By week two, Terry from Totton went for a Burton when he revealed that he liked to go angling in women's clothes.

Nigel and Ray seemed promising.

Nigel, tall, silvery, handsome, was in the armed forces. He had one last upcoming tour of duty and wanted to meet her before he left. His emails were like poetry. He was already talking about their shared future together, where they would live, how they would spend their retirement. Just looking at his picture made her heart swoon.

Ray had thinning dark hair. Glasses, a kind smile, ordinary-looking. Vaguely familiar, she thought she had seen him around Chandler's Ford. His emails were gentle, funny. He was a widower with two children. Enjoyed cycling. He alluded to her photograph, mentioning her lovely skin, beautiful hair.

Another Friday night. She and Joan sat inside. The nights were drawing in.

'Ask to meet them,' Joan suggested.

'I suppose I could suggest coffee…'

'Go for it, girl!'

Next morning, her inbox pinged. An email from Nigel with lots of crying-face emojis, kisses, a poem. His tour of duty was being pulled forward. He was leaving for the Middle East tomorrow and would be in touch.

Hmm, she thought, smelling a rat.

A reply from Ray suggested they met at the King Rufus next Saturday.

Irene was dumbstruck. What was she doing? She could never meet Ray. He thought she looked like the photo but she looked nothing like it now. This whole thing had been a mistake. She didn't need this. She didn't need anyone. Her life was fine. What a fool she had been!

Thirty minutes later, Joan's heels clacked as she bustled around Irene's kitchen.

'Too early for a glass of wine?'

Irene nodded.

'Would you like to meet Ray?' Joan slurped her tea. 'If so, email him to say that, ahem, a couple of years have passed since the photo was taken. But he will still recognise you.'

'What will he think of me?'

'You won't be the first or last to post an outdated photo on a dating site. He might even have done it himself.'

'He's too straightforward to do that.'

Bolstered by her friend's encouragement, Irene emailed Ray. She felt a fuzzy glow when he replied immediately to say he was still looking forward to meeting her.

"I will bring the Financial Times and a red rose to help you recognise me," he had written.

The King Rufus was quiet on Saturday afternoon. A few football fans. A young couple. She prowled the rooms. There was only one man sitting on his own, in a quiet corner. He looked up. Spectacles, round face, bald head. He looked familiar somehow. But where was Ray?

The man stood up. A lop-sided smile, a rose, a pink newspaper.

'Irene.'

'Ray? You're the man from the Science Centre!'

'I liked you that night. Then I recognised your photo on the dating site.'

Irene blinked.

'I knew how shy you were. Knew I had to be patient.'

Irene was enveloped by the scent of warm woody aftershave as he stepped towards her.

'But... you look nothing like your photo!'

His face fell.

'I'm sorry, Irene. The thought of dating again was so daunting. I look ancient. I thought no one would want me so I put an old photo on the website.' He reached towards her.

She pushed his hands away.

'How could you not let me know we had already met?'

'Please, please forgive me. I half-hoped you might recognise me from the Science Centre, like I recognised you. Everything else is true. It was just the photo...'

His eyes were beseeching, his smile tentative. She felt a rush of empathy. It *was* intimidating to feel shy, old.

'I suppose I cheated with my photo as well.'

They smiled at each other.

'Let's have that coffee.'

Wedding Day

Maggie Farran

Five months before her wedding, Chloe finally plucked up the courage to tell her Mum what she really felt. The invitations were due to go out in a couple of weeks. After that, it would be too late to change plans.

Chloe made her Mum a cup of tea and sat down beside her at the kitchen table. She looked round the beautiful kitchen at the family home in Lakewood Road. The gleaming white units were set off by a bright orange glass splash back. The kitchen window looked out over a large garden. Even on this gloomy February day it looked beautiful with the manicured lawn surrounded by trees and shrubs.

'Mum, I need to talk to you about the wedding plans.'

'Oh, there's nothing for you to worry about, dear. Everything is moving along nicely. It's all in hand. I just need to ask you about your bouquet. What colour flowers would you like? I thought shades of pink would go well with the bridesmaids' dresses.'

'Please, Mum, listen to me for once. It's not about flowers matching dresses or how many guests we should invite. I don't want a big church wedding at Saint Boniface and a huge reception at the Hilton. I want a small celebration with family and a few close friends.' Chloe flushed. She couldn't believe what she had said.

'Don't be ridiculous, darling. It's just last minute nerves. Of course you want a proper wedding. You don't want a skimpy little wedding like Dad and I were forced to have. It was such a disappointment for me. There wasn't any money around twenty-five years ago for anything grander. It's so different for you. Dad and I can afford to pay for a really gorgeous wedding, a wedding that will fill you and Chris with pride.'

Chloe never thought about her mother's wedding. She'd seen her parent's wedding photo on top of the highly polished grand piano. They both looked happy and so very young. It had been twenty-five years ago after all. Her mother, Maureen, was dressed in a white dress and her father, Colin, wore a slightly tight traditional suit. She had always assumed that her mother had adored her wedding day.

'What do you mean, Mum? I didn't know you were disappointed with your wedding. I always thought you had enjoyed your day.'

'I don't like to talk about it, darling. It sounds so ungrateful. Everything was done on the cheap. My parents did the best they could. It was a very small wedding at the local church with a reception for close relatives in the church hall. I bought my dress in a sale. I wasn't even allowed to invite my friends. Don't get me wrong I was so happy to be marrying your Dad. I'd always imagined my wedding day as a fairy tale, since I was a little girl. The reality was a bit of a disappointment.'

Chloe bit her lip and put her arm round her mum. She kissed

her on the cheek.

'Mum, I know you are trying so hard to give me what you think I want. It isn't last minute nerves. I'm so different from you. That's what you've got to understand. I really don't want a big posh wedding. Chris and I just want a small 'do'. We are both quite private people. Strangely enough the wedding you had would suit us down to the ground.'

Her mum started to cry. Chloe passed her a tissue.

'I'm sorry, Mum. I don't want to upset you. It's better that I tell you the truth now.'

'What do you mean you're sorry? You don't realise how much I've been looking forward to this day. I've spent hours planning every detail to make it perfect for you. How can you be so ungrateful?'

Her mother stormed out of the room banging into the piano as she went. Chloe picked up her parent's wedding photo, which had fallen onto the carpet. She studied the photo intently looking for clues to try to understand how she and her mother were so different.

Her mother loved her beautiful house and her large garden. It had always been her ambition to live in Lakewood Road. Her parents had both worked hard to achieve the lifestyle they wanted. They had managed to buy a house in one of the most expensive areas of Chandler's Ford. Her mother loved entertaining and was a marvellous hostess. She was so much more extrovert than her. Everyone in their road knew her and appeared to like her.

Chloe walked into the garden and found her father busy in the greenhouse thinning out his seedlings.

'Dad, I've upset Mum. She's flounced off in a temper.'

'What have you said to her, dear? You know how careful we have to be when we are talking to your Mum. She's so excited about your wedding.'

'It's about the wedding. I don't want a great big wedding. I just want a little 'do'. I hate being the centre of attention.'

'I know, love. You're more like me. You don't like fuss. Don't worry; I'll have a word with her. I've got a little plan that should keep her happy.'

Chloe kissed her Dad on the top of his bald head, 'Thanks, Dad.'

He squeezed her hand with his gardening glove.

Chloe walked down to the bottom of the garden and sat on her old swing, which her Dad had hung on the oak tree all those years ago when she was a young girl. She swung gently backwards and forwards and thought about the contrast between her mother's childhood and her own. Her mother had grown up the oldest of four children in a poor area of Southampton. She hadn't had many clothes or toys. All the money had gone on food and rent. Whereas her childhood had been completely different. She had always lived in a beautiful home, worn fashionable clothes and the latest toys had been bought for her. She could understand why her mother wanted a wedding for her that she had not been able to afford for herself. She got down from the swing and walked slowly into the kitchen.

Her mother was busy preparing the evening meal. She moved swiftly and efficiently chopping the vegetables and setting the table.

'Mum, the table looks lovely. You always make such an effort even when it's only the three of us.'

'I enjoy setting the table. What's the point in having lovely things if you don't use them?' she replied curtly.

'Mum, I'm not criticising. I like it that you take such care with everything. I know I'm lucky to live in this house and to have a mother that loves me.'

Her mother put down the placemats and smiled at her. Chloe walked over and gave her a hug.

'I'm sorry, Mum. I know you would be brilliant at organising a big, posh wedding. It's just not what I want.'

'It's me who should be apologising to you. Thinking back, all this planning has been about me and what I wanted. I haven't really been thinking about you at all. Of course you should have the sort of wedding you want. We'll just have a few guests. We'll have your wedding in our garden if that's what you would like.'

'Oh I'd love that, Mum. Thanks for being so understanding. I know we are very different. I never wanted to upset you.'

Her Mum gave her a hug, 'I know you didn't, dear.'

On her wedding day in June the sun shone. Chloe stood in the garden with her arm around Chris. 'Thanks, Dad, for working so hard on the garden. The roses look perfect. This really has been the best day of my life. It's the perfect little family wedding that Chris and I wanted.'

Her Dad smiled. 'I'm glad you got the wedding you wanted, love. You know your Mum missed out on her own wedding. I've planned a surprise for her on our Silver Wedding in August. Keep it a secret. I'm taking her away on one of those Mediterranean cruises. She will be able to dress up every evening in one of those long frocks. '

Chloe laughed. 'You better not leave it a secret too long, Dad. Mum will need at least a couple of months to buy all the dresses she needs. A different gown for each evening of the cruise, I should think.'

Tea for Two

Catherine Griffin

Lauren paused outside Bay Leaves Larder to check her reflection in the glass door. With a quick sweep of her fingers, she brushed her long brown hair back from her face.

Although she'd lived in Chandler's Ford for several years, she hadn't been into this coffee shop before. She didn't know why Donald had chosen it, but his text message had been clear about the time and place.

She pushed the door open.

A pleasant buzz of chatter, chinking china, and the smell of food welcomed her inside. She scanned the room, but none of the customers seated at the wooden tables were Donald. The flutter in her stomach subsided into disappointment. He must be running late. No doubt he'd be here soon. She made her way towards an empty table.

A middle-aged lady who had been sitting alone at a table stood, blocking Lauren's path. She looked Lauren up and down coolly.

'Are you Lauren?'

Lauren blinked. The round pale woman with her Paisley scarf

and strong floral perfume was a complete stranger. Perhaps they'd met at the Blue Cross centre, or through work, and she'd forgotten. That seemed more likely than being accosted by someone she'd never met, so she smiled, hoping the name would come to her in a moment.

The woman didn't smile back. 'I'm Kay.'

Still no bells. Lauren couldn't recall meeting or hearing about anyone named Kay.

'I'm sorry. Should I know you?'

Kay's lips quirked into a tight smile. 'Sit down. We should talk.'

Lauren glanced at the table, at the empty chair.

'Sorry, I'm here to meet someone.'

She tried to step past, but ran into Kay's fleshy arm.

'I know. I'm Donald's wife.'

Lauren froze, her heart jammed into her throat. *Donald's wife.* He'd talked about his wife. She'd known she existed. But she'd never expected to speak to her, and certainly not under these circumstances.

Kay steered her, unprotesting, into the free chair at the table. They sat facing each other.

'I had a message,' Lauren said, 'from Donald.'

'I borrowed his phone.'

Lauren's mouth went dry. If Kay had sent the text message, had she seen the messages Lauren had sent Donald? She didn't think she'd said anything too indiscreet. Maybe a bit flirty.

'Why...?'

'I wanted to meet you and it seemed the simplest way. Do you want tea? Coffee?'

'Green tea, please,' Lauren said numbly.

Kay got up and went to order from the counter, leaving Lauren to pull herself together.

Donald had described his wife as cold and distant. They were divorcing, he said. The vague picture Lauren had built in her head couldn't be reconciled with Kay's cool, straightforward manner, nor with the underhand way she'd been lured to this meeting. She ought to go. Lauren willed herself to get up and walk out of the door, but her legs wouldn't move. It was like a nightmare.

Kay returned.

'Now, you must be wondering what all this is about. I'm sorry if the text message misled you. I just thought we should have a short chat. Sort some things out, you know?'

Lauren felt like her brain was melting. In the real world, this sort of thing surely didn't happen. If Kay was shouting and screaming it would be easier to understand.

'The thing is,' Kay said, 'it won't work.'

'It won't?'

'I'm often away from home on business, and Donald works long hours. He has too soft a heart. That's always been his problem. He doesn't think things through, and it's always up to me to sort out the mess. I'm sorry if you hoped otherwise, but I'm sure you can understand my point of view.'

'Uh... I'm not sure I quite see...'

'Well, I know you want the best for the animals. It wouldn't be fair, would it? A dog shouldn't be alone all day.'

Lauren shuddered in relief. The dog. Of course. Donald had been talking about adopting a dog from the centre. She wasn't sure if it was serious or just an excuse to see her. The text messages they'd exchanged, a lot of them had been about possible dogs. And his visits to her... he must have told his wife it was to look at dogs. It all made sense now.

'Of course, yes. I quite understand. You're absolutely right.'

She was babbling, she realised. The waitress arrived with two cups of tea, and Lauren was glad of the distraction to get her thoughts in order. She cradled her cup in her hands, enjoying the familiar scent. Kay sipped her tea, eyeing Lauren calmly.

The overwhelming relief faded. Was this just about the dog or was there more to it? How much did Kay know?

'Obviously, I'm disappointed,' Lauren said carefully. 'I thought Donald was really interested. In having a dog.'

'He gets these ideas sometimes. People misunderstand, but it isn't serious. He feels sorry for the waifs and strays, lets his heart override his head.'

Lauren pushed her tea away.

'If that was all you had to say, I think I should go. I have an appointment...'

Before she could stand, Kay's hand shot across the table to grab her wrist.

'Do you mind?'

Lauren didn't want to make a scene, but Kay's twisted face and the grip on her wrist suggested a scene was going to happen whether she liked it or not.

'Sit down,' Kay hissed. 'I haven't finished with you yet.'

Lauren folded back into the chair, and Kay released her wrist.

'Just listen,' Kay said. 'I'm not going to beat around the bush any more. We both know exactly what's going on here. Did you really think you were the first?'

Lauren stirred, aware of the hardness of the chair against her legs and back, the multitude of tables between her and the door. Shock and guilt held her pinned before the older woman's gaze.

'I bet he made puppy-dog eyes at you and whined how his wife doesn't understand him. I know. I know exactly how it goes. How long?'

Lauren flinched. 'Not long. Just...'

It had started when Donald brought a stray dog into the centre. He'd nearly run it over in the street. Was so upset, so caring. Had hung around, looking at the dogs and chatting. The next day he came back to check on the dog. Then he started talking about maybe adopting one. He'd taken her to a pub and they'd talked all afternoon. They had so much in common.

'... a few weeks.'

Kay nodded. 'It won't last. A couple of months, at most. Then he'll be sobbing on my shoulder, telling me how sorry he is.'

Lauren stared. 'How many?'

'I stopped counting.' Kay gulped at her tea.

There were tears in her eyes, and Lauren felt a sudden surge of sympathy for her.

'Why? Why don't you leave him? Why would you put up with being treated like that?'

Kay rubbed the heel of her hand across her eyes. She laughed weakly.

'Stupid. I'm stupid and weak. Look at me.'

Lauren stretched across the table to take her hand. 'Don't say that. You aren't stupid.'

'I love him. I know what he is and still love him. How stupid is that?'

'Nothing's happened,' Lauren said. 'Not really. I mean, we

talked, we flirted. That's all, I swear.'

Kay sniffed. 'Thank you. I'm sorry. I shouldn't have done this. I was angry and I wanted... I don't know what I wanted.'

'I'm glad you did. He told me he was married. I should have walked away then, I should have known better.'

Lauren felt light-headed. It didn't hurt yet. When it sank in, there would be tears and anger and eating a whole tub of ice cream in one go, but for now there was only numbness and clarity. She could see the road she would have travelled laid out before her, with all the pleasure and the pain, and she was being given a chance to stop, and choose the better path.

'Thank you.' She squeezed Kay's hand.

The older woman was no longer looking at her. Her attention was fixed over Lauren's shoulder, towards the door. Lauren twisted in her seat to see Donald, staring at them both in shock and horror.

Slimming Club

Maggie Farran

Susie leapt off the scales and screamed.

'That can't be right. There must be something wrong with the scales.'

She stepped on again carefully and breathed in. She looked down at the dial. She looked at herself in the mirror, really staring instead of the usual brief glance.

There was no doubt about it, she was fat.

She wasn't chubby or well-built or big-boned. She was just plain fat. How had she let this happen?

When she'd first had her daughter, everyone had said the weight would drop off with all those disturbed nights and breastfeeding. It wasn't true. Isabel was two, and Susie weighed more now than in the last month of pregnancy.

There was, if she was honest, no real mystery about it. She thought of all those delicious cakes she'd eaten at Kelly's Coffee Shop, where she met with the other mums. All the toast and jam she'd eaten in the middle of the night when Isabel refused to sleep. The Saturday night Chinese take-away from Canton House, washed down by copious amounts of red wine.

'Nigel, I'm going to the slimming club on Monday evening. I can't go on like this.'

Nigel tore his attention from the TV and frowned at her. 'Are you sure, Susie love? You look fine, cuddly and gorgeous.'

'I don't want to be cuddly, Nige. I want to be slim and elegant,' she said a little more fiercely than she meant.

'I like cuddly.' Nigel turned back to the TV and his bag of crisps.

Before she set out on Monday Susie tucked into a big cream cake she'd bought from Waitrose. She'd chosen it with care and ate it slowly, savouring every last sugary mouthful.

Nigel watched her with a sly smile.

'Is that your last supper then Suze?'

'You could call it that. It's going to be a long time before I can have another cream cake.'

The hall was packed. Apart from one man, it was full of women of all different sizes. Several people were enormous, but otherwise they were like her with a stone or two to lose.

Susie took off her shoes and earrings before she was weighed. There was no point in adding ounces. She shivered in her light summer dress.

'Just hop up onto the scales and then I'll give you a target weight. Here is our booklet explaining all about our new weight loss programme. I'll talk to you after the meeting and explain everything. I'm Becky by the way. I'm your leader.'

Becky had one of those irritating over-bright voices and

reminded Susie of one of those girls from her hockey team at school.

Susie sat down and wondered how long it was going to take to lose two whole stone. How many months was she going to have to live on lettuce and tomatoes?

Becky came to the front and asked brightly 'How has everyone got on in the last week?'

It was a bit like being back at school with the goody-goodies answering all the questions. One woman was particularly annoying. She had lost 5 pounds in a week and seemed to have studied the programme as if she were taking a degree. Becky gave them a recipe for low calorie Spaghetti Bolognese. She told them that she made large quantities and froze the rest in individual portions. Susie and Nigel never seemed to have any leftovers to freeze.

The following day Susie took Isabel to meet up with another mum, Emily and her toddler. Susie sat and ate her banana while Emily tucked into a large slice of cheesecake.

'What's the matter, Susie? It's not like you to choose the healthy option. You're not trying to lose weight are you? '

Susie looked at Emily. She was so slim. No one would think she'd ever had a baby. It just wasn't fair.

'It's alright for you. You can eat what you like. I'm trying to lose a couple of stone.'

'You're fine, Susie. You're just a curvy girl. Here, have a little bit of mine.'

Her friend cut her cheesecake in half and passed it to her. It would be rude to refuse, thought Susie. It tasted delicious.

Susie cooked two fish fingers and baked beans for Isabel's supper. Isabel took one look and buttoned up her little mouth.

'Come on, Isabel, eat a little bit. You like fish fingers. At least you did yesterday.'

Isabel now seemed to hate them with a vengeance. Susie managed to shovel the beans into Isabel's stubborn mouth. The fish fingers somehow managed to find themselves being eaten by Susie.

In the evening she cooked the slimmer's version of Spaghetti Bolognese for herself and Nigel.

'Is that the size of your portion, Susie? It doesn't even look enough for a child.' He laughed. 'Here have a bit of mine.'

He shovelled some on her plate before she could stop him. She didn't want to waste it. It was so tasty. He was being thoughtful.

It was a week later when Susie got out of the shower. She dried every last drop of water from her naked body before she stepped on the scales.

It couldn't be true. She had only lost one miserable pound.

'It's not fair, Nigel. I've practically starved myself all week. I've only lost a pound.'

Nigel went slightly pink. 'Well you have cheated a bit, darling.'

'What do you mean? When have I cheated?'

'You had that apple crumble on Sunday and that cream cake yesterday.'

'Oh shut up, Nigel. Are you a member of the food police?'

Susie knew it was true. She had tried to keep to her diet, but it was just so hard. She loved cakes and puddings. The lady from the slimming club had suggested sugar-free jelly with fruit. She'd tried it once, but it didn't compare to a chocolate éclair or a jam doughnut.

That night at the meeting Susie felt embarrassed to be weighed but she was made to feel quite a success.

'Brilliant, Susie, you've made a really good start. The first pound is always the hardest. If you lose a steady pound a week you'll be at your target weight in thirty weeks. That's only seven months or so.' Becky smiled.

Susie went home quite jubilant and had a Crunchie to celebrate. After all, she had another week before she was going to be weighed again. She decided she was going to do some extra exercise this week as well as eating healthy food. It was so easy to plan this while she sprawled on the sofa relishing her chocolate bar.

She got up early the next morning and pulled on her new exercise gear. After dropping Isabel off at playgroup she drove to 3d Fitness. It had been years since she'd been to an exercise class. It was a bit of a struggle. Retired women were managing better than she was. She stood at the back and could see her face in the wall mirrors getting steadily redder and redder. She looked like a plump tomato just ready to be picked. Still, she completed the class and the instructor was encouraging.

For the next few weeks, she kept to her healthy eating plan. She went to 3d Fitness on the three mornings a week that Isabel was at playgroup. Every week she lost a pound or two.

'You're doing so well, Susie. You've had a steady weight loss.

You've only got a couple of pounds to lose before you reach your goal weight.'

These last two pounds were a nightmare to lose. Susie didn't let anything pass her lips that weren't on her healthy eating plan. She put all her effort into her exercise classes. When she looked in the wall mirrors now she was pleased with what she saw. Her face was a normal colour. She wasn't bursting out of her gym clothes.

She felt so much more positive. She had so much more energy when she played with Isabel. Nigel showered her with compliments. He couldn't keep his hands off her. It was just like the early days of their marriage. He even bought her some delicate lacy underwear.

'I can't wait to see you in these, Suze. They'll show off your beautiful, sexy, body.'

Susie laughed but she was secretly thrilled. She felt young and attractive again.

In fact, Susie wasn't at all surprised when she went for her regular weigh-in and Becky said, 'You seem to have put a couple of pounds on this week. Don't let it upset you though. You've done so well.'

Susie beamed at her. 'I'm not upset at all. I'm pregnant. I'm going to have a baby in six months' time.'

'Congratulations, but remember no eating for two this time round,' said Becky with a knowing wink.

Too Late to Party

Karen Stephen

Zelda nuzzled the Pekinese nestling in her arms. Chou Chou's tongue flicked. 'Walkies?'

Chou Chou's ears didn't perk up as normal. Her stubby tail wagged only once.

'Are you sick, my darling?'

Zelda held Chou Chou in front of her. Chou Chou's eyes had lost their merry sparkle. The dog looked ill.

In her apartment in Sutherland Drive, under the watchful gaze of her children's portraits, Zelda pondered.

'We'll go to your favourite vet, Chou Chou. Afterwards, Mummy will meet Jonny at the Halfway Inn as usual.'

Zelda opened her wardrobe.

'I need to make a statement.' Chou Chou lay listless on the floor. 'Must keep the show on the road.'

Dressed in black skirt and scarlet jacket, she applied make-up in front of the gilt-edged mirror. A sip of wine stilled the shaking of her hands.

She drew on arched eyebrows. She smacked her lips together to smooth the Crimson Madam lipstick. She was running low on her favourite colour. She would buy a replacement, cut back on something else this week.

In the drawer she found a sequinned jet-black beret. She positioned it at a jaunty angle.

Immediately she was transported to Costa Smeralda, 1979. She was 23. Crisp white beaches. Lazy days on yachts. The fast crowd which she hung around with. Long nights of dancing at Studio 42. Gerald Del Castelvecchio. It was Gerald she remembered most of all. Tall, dark, dashing. He had told her he was rich, promised her the world...

Chou Chou yelped. Dazed, Zelda returned to the present. For a second, she wondered who the shadowy old woman in the dusty mirror was. She sucked in her cheeks. Pouted.

'Mummy's still got it, hasn't she? Let's party!'

Outside, traffic roared. Scooping the dog into her arms, Zelda clip-clopped towards the bus stop. A youth barged past on a skateboard. A cyclist almost knocked her over.

'You shouldn't be on the pavement, you oafs!' she shouted.

The cyclist flipped a finger at her.

A fat family waddled in front of her. Disapproval settled around her like a cloak.

'They need to take a leaf out my book, Chou Chou. I haven't had a full meal since 1986.' She looked at her slender arms. Her slim, elegant hands tapered into long cherry-polished nails. She frowned, deciding to ignore the wrinkles, age-spots.

The vet's premises were the last building in the dirty, grey precinct of takeaways, nail salons. She used her sleeve to open the door to avoid touching the smudgy fingerprints.

'You again?' The receptionist sighed.

Zelda shuddered when she noticed her tattoos. What was it with young people these days?

'Chou Chou is sick. I insist she sees the vet immediately.'

The receptionist sighed again. She tapped her screen.

'First appointment he's got is at four.'

Zelda felt a throb of irritation. She had a date with Jonny this afternoon at the Halfway Inn.

'That's not acceptable. It's a priority. I want to see Mr Oldcastle at once.'

'Won't happen. Sorry.'

Zelda sucked air into her lungs. Stretched her shoulders, arched her back.

'Why don't you,' she tapped a nail on the desk, 'buzz him now? Tell him Zelda's here.'

Tattoo-girl flicked greasy hair from her face. She stared at Zelda with a glassy-eyed look of disdain.

Chou Chou mewled.

'There, there, darling. This girl is being obstreperous. Mr Oldcastle will be furious when I tell him about this.'

The receptionist pointed to a sign on a counter.

'"Any person abusing the staff will be ejected." How dare you?'

'Like I said, the vet can see you at four.'

Zelda made a quick calculation.

'Too late to go home, Chou Chou. We'll go to the pub and come back.'

Halfway Inn was crowded with the lunch-time throng. Zelda shrunk at the sight of the tradesmen. Big, smelly oafs who drank beer, watched football, leered at women.

'Yoohoo! Over here Zelda.' Jonny was in his usual corner. 'Love the sequinned beret. You look good enough to eat, sweetie!'

For the first time today, Zelda smiled, relaxed. She settled Chou Chou on her lap.

'You look gorgeous too. I love the pink.' He looked fetching in white slacks, salmon-coloured sweater, fuchsia cravat.

'Let's start with bubbles.' He started towards the bar. Turned. 'I seem to have forgotten my wallet. Could you just…'

'Silly sausage. You'll forget who you are one day.' Zelda gave him her purse. 'You're worth it. You remind me of the old days.'

The Babycham flowed. They laughed. They reminisced. The afternoon blurred.

'Look at the time!' It was nearly four.

Mwahing goodbye to Jonny, Zelda scuttled from the pub clutching Chou Chou.

In the late afternoon gloom, car lights glared through the rain. Zelda rushed across the busy intersection.

'Are you alright, lady?'

Hands pulled at Zelda. She seemed to be lying on the road. Her mouth felt wet, gritty. Her ankle throbbed. Chou Chou was curled up in a ball.

She hauled herself up. Traffic whizzed past. Horns honked.

'OK, love?'

She limped past her burly rescuers. Exhaled with relief when she saw the vet's.

As she waited, she did her best to smooth her clothes. Chou Chou snuggled in her arms, none the worse for the fall.

A buzzer rang. Chou Chou's name flashed on the board.

'What's going on?' The vet gestured them into the room.

Zelda looked around his office. Family portraits peered from the walls.

'Chou Chou isn't well.'

'I mean with you, Zelda.'

How tall he was. How handsome still.

'Look at you, Zelda.'

Zelda glimpsed her torn tights, broken finger nails.

'You're drunk again. What a ridiculous hat!'

Her mouth felt full of jagged nails.

'Gerald, please…' She glanced at the photographs. Happier times. Chou Chou as a puppy. Their children.

'I know I wasn't what you expected. Life wasn't what you wanted.' He sounded sad.

'You promised me the world. You sold me a lie!'

'I promised you Gerald Oldcastle. But you set your heart on Gerald Del Castelvechhio. You wouldn't accept reality.'

Zelda Oldcastle felt a tear roll down her cheek.

'The party's over. It's not 1979.' He plucked the sequinned beret from her head. 'You need to grow up, Zelda.' He sighed, ran his hands through his silvered-hair. 'Before it's too late.'

The Last Tree

Sally Howard

I'm not a fighter.

I'm lying before the jaws of a bright yellow bulldozer. I shift uncomfortably as the chill of damp mud seeps through my parka. I pull it tighter over my fluffy dressing gown. My breath mists in the milky dawn air. I think of what Mum always says to me:

'You're not a fighter.'

Last week I agreed with her on this point.

'What!' Mum dropped her tablet on the kitchen counter. It skidded and bounced on the floor. It's one of those new polymer plastic ones they developed for the Mars expeditions. Take a truck to trash it, as the advert says.

Anyway, Mum was spluttering into her coffee. 'Proposed further housing development in Chandler's Ford!'

I took away her mug before any more brown milky liquid sloshed down the side of the cabinet, to pool next to the tablet on the floor.

'Houses allowed up to eight storeys high.' Her voice rose

107

several octaves.

This type of challenge is bread and butter for Mum.

Both Mum and Dad are fighters. Apparently they fought to make this place a better place, a safer place. They don't tell me how exactly. A knowing smile tweaks at Dad's mouth whenever they talk about those days and he squeezes Mum's arm. And she encourages him.

Yulch. Teenagers shouldn't have to put up with this type of parental behaviour.

Anyway, Mum retrieved the tablet from the puddle and stabbed at the screen.

'Plans include demolishing the oak tree by the pond. Can you believe it? Our last tree!'

That was her red flag. She wasted no time. She picked up the phone, called her contacts, mobilised the troops.

As I listened to her rattling on, I stared out the window. What would it be like when the houses at the back were built higher?

The delicate saplings in our garden already looked a bit yellow. They're beginning to bend over, fighting for a meagre share of sun from the six-storey houses over the fence. Will they even survive if — no — *when* they remove the roofs on those houses and add on another couple of storeys?

It's inevitable. Building up is the only option. No more green space left. Every little patch filled in with housing. In fact, we're lucky to have resisted for so long. My breath mists the window. The buildings become a tall blurry outline.

The next morning, I set off extra early to the bus stop, thinking to stop off at the oak tree, perhaps get something for Mum, find some token that she could remember the tree by or maybe put a ribbon around the trunk. I don't know what. It's just a thought really. Probably a silly idea. Risky even.

The old oak next to the pond is encircled by a low fence. I push the gate open and sit on the bench. A light breeze ruffles the rushes round the pond. In the middle, the resident heron sits imperiously on a tufted clump of grass, oblivious to the encroaching bricks and mortar on all sides.

The breeze stirs the first green shoots of spring leaves along the branches. I'm surprised at these shoots. The tree, like the mistress of a bygone age, seems too old for this youthful display. The gnarled, twisted branches, like too-heavy arms, lean on the ground. Ivy wraps like a skirt around her spreading waist. Her bark, dark brown and fissured with age, is criss-crossed with lesions which weep dark fluid. Rotting from within, she has succumbed to Acute Oak Disease.

The council will pull her down, before she falls of her own accord.

I stretch and yawn. It's pleasant though, sitting here so early.

I hear it before I see it. The high pitched buzz of a drone. It drops out of the sky in front of me.

Tiny blades whip round in a blur at the end of grey Meccano arms. A door on the underside opens and a small screen snaps into place.

'Consumer,' says a thin, metallic voice. 'Do you have a garden for hire?'

Images of lush lawns, well-stocked flower beds, and fruit-laden trees flash across the screen.

'We have families in need of access to green areas,' it continues. 'Favourable rates paid for suitable gardens. All times considered.

Top prices for Sundays and Bank Holidays. Call… Give Us Yer Garden.com.'

The drone hangs in the air, swaying from side to side like a plump bumblebee.

'Go away.' I wave at it, before it can start another advert.

The screen flickers again, this time rolling images of econo-pod housing. Like I want any of this stuff.

It clicks and whirrs and pushes out a leaflet which floats gently onto my lap. I'm about to crumple the eco-paper and let it disperse on the breeze, when I hear more buzzing. I look up. The sky is overcast with drones. The first drone has acted like a beacon, attracting others from all around.

'Go away,' I shout.

Too late, they're dropping from the sky like a curtain of rain. Surrounding me. Stupid. I thought I'd be safe under the tree, but instead I'm a sitting duck.

Dozens of screens snap open. Metallic voices all begin at once: 'Consumer... Consumer...' The volume increases to a shrill fever pitch, as each one tries to outdo the next. I clamp my hands over my ears.

Drones buzz around me like hornets. I duck my head and run for the gate. My bag slaps hard against my back. A drone flits in close, vying for my attention. Its razor-sharp wings catch my cheek. I cry out, press my hand to my face, feel blood warm and sticky on my fingers, metallic on my lips.

'This way!' A hand pulls my arm and guides me forward.

A stick swipes at the drones. Two fall to the ground, wings clipped. Their tiny motors spark, sending slivers of acrid smoke into the air.

I slip my bag off my shoulder and swing at a drone. Amazingly I hit it. I go in for another. Out of the corner of my eye I see him swipe with his tree branch. Several drones lie dead on the ground. We run for the bus shelter.

The remaining drones lift into the air, as if they can sense danger.

I fall into the safety of the shelter and lean against the polymer plastic window, heart thumping, gasping, laughing.

'OK?' he says.

I look up, into the brown eyes of Josh from the year above me. We stare at each other for a moment. He reaches out and tilts my head.

'Your cheek, it's bleeding.'

He dabs at it with a tissue. Clean, I hope.

I get to have a good look at his face up close. Straight nose. Dimple in his chin. His brow is furrowed. Is that with concern, I wonder? I hope.

I realise he's stopped cleaning my face. I've been caught staring at him. I drop my head.

'Thanks for your help,' I mutter.

'Bit silly being out there in a public space like that.'

I snap my head up. 'Well, I'm sorry. I thought it was safe under the tree. I was only gonna be a moment.'

'It's not safe anywhere. You should know that by now.'

'I do. You don't need to remind me, thank you!'

Cheeks burning, I stomp off to the other side of the shelter. So that's how it is. He thinks I'm just some swoony little kid. My elation drains and I slump against the shelter. My cheek throbs like I've been stung by a bee.

He comes over, hands stuck in his pockets. 'I think we got off on the wrong foot. I'm Josh.'

'I'm Becky Champion.'

He raises an eyebrow. 'As in the Champions? Your parents are Mr and Mrs Champion?'

'Yes.'

'Cool.'

He goes quiet. What's he thinking? I start to fidget, playing with a cigarette butt under my shoe. Birds have resumed their morning song now the drones have gone. Soon the bus shelter will fill with other students. How can I break the awkward silence?

I look down at the leaflet I still clutch in my hand. I'm about to crumple it, when he takes it from me and smooths it against his jeans.

'This is one of ours.'

'One of yours?'

He passes it back to me. I read: 'Rally at the Old Oak. Save our last tree.'

I look up at him. 'But the tree's dying anyway. If we don't take it down, it'll fall down.'

'Possibly. But there are treatments for the disease. If you want to spend the money. But more importantly...' A smile curves his lips. 'More importantly, there are seedlings growing round the base of the tree. The old oak will protect them as they grow.'

'Oh. I didn't see them.'

'I was on my way to check on them, when I saw you, surrounded, as it were, by your swarm of admirers.'

'Pesky flies, more like.'

'Flies round a honey-pot,' he says and smiles.

112

This morning, I was woken by thumping at the front door. The bulldozers had arrived early, sneaking in, trying to rip down the old tree ahead of time and make a done deal of it. No time to lose, I slung my parka over my dressing gown. Josh and I raced down the road to join his friends, holding the fort round the tree.

Now, I lie here, in front of this bright yellow bulldozer, an arm's length from Josh, not at all minding the chill of damp mud seeping through my parka. I think of what Mum has always said to me:

'You're not a fighter... until you've found something worth fighting for.'

Afterword

Since publishing our first collection of short stories, **Secret Lives of Chandlers Ford,** we've talked to hundreds of Chandler's Ford people we wouldn't otherwise have met. We've had help and support from shopkeepers, librarians, and historians. **More Secret Lives of Chandlers Ford** is dedicated to all the lovely Chandler's Ford folk who inspire us to keep writing.

We hope you enjoyed reading this book. If you did, or even if you didn't, please take a moment to leave your honest review on Amazon. Whether it's one star or five, reviews help authors and other readers. You can also get in touch with us via our Facebook page (Secret Lives of Chandlers Ford) or Twitter (@chfordlives).

This book would not have been possible without the support and help of Barbara Large and our fellow Creative Writing students. If you are reading this, thank you!

Made in the USA
Charleston, SC
13 November 2016